# Unwelcome Settlers

**Center Point
Large Print**

**This Large Print Book carries the
Seal of Approval of N.A.V.H.**

# Unwelcome Settlers

## ROBERT J. HORTON

CENTER POINT PUBLISHING
THORNDIKE, MAINE

This Center Point Large Print edition
is published in the year 2006 by arrangement with
Golden West Literary Agency.

The text of this Large Print edition is unabridged. In other
aspects, this book may vary from the original edition. Printed in
Thailand. Set in 16-point Times New Roman type.

ISBN 1-58547-805-9

Library of Congress Cataloging-in-Publication Data

Horton, Robert J., d. 1934.
    Unwelcome settlers / Robert J. Horton.--Center Point large print ed.
      p. cm.
    ISBN 1-58547-805-9 (lib. bdg. : alk. paper)
    1. Large type books.  I. Title.

PS3515.O745U59 2006
813'.52--dc22

2006003321

# CONTENTS

# CHAPTER I
## INTO THE SUNSET

THE new-born town of Angel glowed like a splash of gold upon the gray surface of the plain, as its clusters of rough, unpainted buildings and drab-colored tents caught the reflection of the sunset in the high skies above the mountains toward the west.

A streamer of smoke trailed against the southern skyline as a train raced northward across the prairies. It pulled up at the bright new station, with its cinder-bedded platform, and disgorged its passengers with a semblance of the haste and excitement which marked all the activities of the homestead rush.

"New West Hotel?" bawled an angular individual from Missouri, who had been one of the first to answer to the call of "free land."

"New West Hotel! Free rig."

Neil Sterret and his wife, Dora, after gazing about at the crudely animated scene for a few seconds, allowed themselves to be escorted to the conveyance which the hotel runner indicated. Other new arrivals crowded in with them, an overflow of baggage was pushed in between their feet, the runner swung up onto the rear step, and they went rattling away over the uneven dirt roads which formed the streets of the town.

At the hotel, which was a two-story wooden building, unpainted and uncarpeted, Neil wrote his name and his wife's on two lines of the bulky register.

"Two rooms," he said to the man behind the desk, "for my sister and me."

The hotel runner, now officiating in the capacity of a bellboy, helped them upstairs with their hand luggage. When he had left the suitcases and grips in their rooms and departed, the girl turned to the man and spoke.

"Why did you say 'sister,' Neil? Now that we are here they are certain to learn sooner or later that we are married."

Neil Sterret dropped into a chair and made a gesture that expressed his disgust. "Hasn't it occurred to you that these people out here in this primitive country would think it strange that a man and his wife should require two rooms? It's the first place we've been where we had to register our names since we left Illinois. The brother-and-sister stuff went without question on the train." He snorted. "Dora, when is this foolishness going to end?"

"Now, Neil, don't let's start that argument all over again," replied the girl, her face flushed.

"Well, it is foolishness, now that we're here," retorted the man heatedly. "What did you marry me for if—"

"For the last time, Neil, I'm going to tell you that I married you because I promised your mother I would, two years ago. You were different then."

"You never loved me, to begin with," complained the husband bitterly.

"Yes, I did," declared Dora, "and I would love you

just as much now if you were the same, but in the two years since your mother died you've changed. You know it. Oh, Neil," she continued, with a sob in her voice, "if you will only make a man of yourself out here I will love you just as much again. When you insisted that I marry you and come out here to the West to your uncle's ranch, where you could make a new start and become a real man, I consented because I wanted you to make good—because I wanted you for my husband if you did make good. Doesn't that show that I cared, and that I'm ready to care again?"

"Don't cry," said Sterret petulantly. "This is a man's country out here, and I'll fit in."

"I hope so," said the girl softly.

The rays of the setting sun, filtering in through the window, gave her hair a rich, golden hue as she removed her hat.

Neil Sterret could not repress an exclamation of admiration as he noted the trim figure of the girl, her flushed cheeks, the glow in her gray eyes under long lashes, the rounded contour of her arms as she raised her hands to put in place stray wisps of hair.

His dark, handsome face, marked with early signs of dissipation, flushed. "But a year, Dora, is a long time," he pleaded.

"It won't seem long when we have a goal to strive for," she replied cheerfully, "and if you make good your promise in a year, we can be really and truly married for a long time."

"What'll Uncle Brodick think?" he countered, frowning.

"Just what we tell him, Neil, and we'll tell him all that he doesn't know now. We'll tell him how your mother looked after me when my parents died, how we fell in love with each other, how your mother wanted us to marry, and how I promised her I would marry you; how you—you—made a few mistakes back in Illinois; how I agreed to your plan to wed and come out West with you, with the understanding that ours was to be a—a formal marriage for a year while you made yourself over out here in this new and splendid environment. Oh, he'll help us, Neil; he'll help you to make good!"

"Well, I'll leave you to do the telling of it, since you made the bargain," said Neil.

"Look!" exclaimed the girl, pointing to the red banners in the sky above the far-flung range of mountains. "It's just as if we'd come right into a sunset, Neil. Isn't it beautiful? No, not beautiful—magnificent, majestic! Neil, back there where we came from we never dreamed there was a country like this. I can feel the change in my very blood; it's tingling already. Don't you sense something like an inspiration?"

"I suppose so," he said, himself impressed with the mighty grandeur of the scene. "Well, let's go down to supper."

Seated at a long table with many others, they ate heartily. There were three long tables in the room, and from one of these tables a large, red-faced man watched them closely during the meal. He followed them out and indicated them with a motion of his thumb to the clerk as they passed into the narrow hallway leading to the stairs. The clerk nodded, and the large man turned on his heel and walked away.

Neil Sterret saw his wife to her room. "I'm going out to look the town over and try to find out if uncle's man is here for us," he said casually.

"You won't get into trouble, Neil? You know, things must be very different out here, and—"

"I can take care of myself," he answered crisply. "Go to bed when you're ready. I'll tap on your door to let you know I'm back when I go to my room."

He stood in her doorway for a time surveying her as she lit the lamp upon the table. He seemed for a moment on the point of advancing across the threshold; then he turned suddenly and stamped down the stairs.

## CHAPTER II
### A NEW CODE

ANGEL'S main street was but dimly lighted, and such illumination as it had came from the stars which dotted the high arch of the heavens overhead. But from the buildings on either side, most of them one-story, hastily-put-together affairs with false fronts, came a faded radiance from kerosene lamps— and the sounds of revelry.

Scores of horses stood at the hitching rails. Some were tied and others stood with drooping heads, the bridle reins dangling free at their feet. The pound of hoofs echoed among sounds of screeching phonographs, tinkling glasses, laughter, shouts, jingling spurs, and the occasional bark of a dog.

Something in the very air—dry, exhilarating, carrying the tang of earth and grass—sensed a new country in the making.

Neil Sterret felt its spell, and his wild blood thrilled to a new sensation. He noted the attire of the men. Most of them wore khaki trousers and shirts. Others appeared in chaps and spurs, with bandanna handkerchiefs about their necks, knotted behind and hanging low in front under the opened bosoms of their shirts. These, too, were armed. Butts of big, black guns protruded from holsters slung low on thighs.

It was with great interest that Neil saw that these men were given plenty of room as they swaggered about with their queer, swaying gait; they seemed to spurn men of less picturesque garb. But the thing that interested him most, perhaps, were the hats these men wore—broad of brim, with a high crown almost invariably dented or pinched in. These big hats seemed a symbol of something which Neil wanted to become—a real Westerner.

He stepped into a store and bought himself such a hat. He was surprised that the huge, gray headgear should feel so easy and light on his head.

"Throw that other thing away," he instructed the

storekeeper with a swagger, pointing to the small, neat, brown fedora which he had worn lately.

Once again he went out into the cool, scented spring night. He walked, this time, to the edge of the town, where he could see the gray reaches of prairie stretching out under a high-hung canopy of stars, to where the black shadow of Angel Butte and the serrated outlines of the higher mountains traced a jagged pattern against the night sky.

He breathed deeply. "Lord, it is a man's country!" he said aloud.

When he returned to the center of town he entered a building whence issued a strange medley of distorted sound. He paused, breathless at the scene.

It was a long, narrow room. Swinging lamps hung from the rough-board ceiling, and other lamps flared from in front of reflectors attached to the walls. On the right side of the room ranged a bar, with glasses and mirrors behind, and, tilted above, so that it was almost over the heads of those who stood drinking their soda pop and "one-half," was a highly colored lithograph of Custer's last fight.

On the left side were arranged a number of tables, about which scores of men were grouped. In the rear was a lunch counter. The air was hazy with tobacco smoke, and the place echoed to the tinkle of glassware, the rattle of money and chips, the squeaking of an ancient music box, and the hoarse laughter and talk and curses of many men.

Neil hesitated a second, walked to the bar, and took

a drink. Next he turned his attention to the tables. His blood leaped when he saw that men were buying chips and gambling them in a strange game. It was the famous "black jack," or "twenty-one," of the West.

Neil saw the dealer shuffle the cards, deal one around the table to each man, one to himself, and repeat the performance. The dealer then looked at his own two cards.

"I'm hittin', boys," he said.

Immediately the various players began to call for cards.

"Hit it!" cried one. "Too many."

The dealer took this man's cards, placed them face up under the balance of the pack he held in his left hand, and raked in the chips the man had wagered.

The next man scraped the table with his two cards, which evidently was a signal that he wished to draw, for the dealer instantly dealt him a card.

"That's good," said the player, and placed his chips upon his cards.

So it continued around the table, some players drawing cards and "staying," others drawing cards and "breaking" and losing their bets, some drawing no cards at all but standing pat on the original two.

Then the dealer began looking at the various hands, taking up all the cards, paying some bets, taking in others, and announcing a stand-off in some cases, in which event he did not take the bet or pay it.

Last of all he exposed his own hand—two face cards.

"Twenty," he announced, and began a new deal.

Neil saw men expose hands consisting of an ace and a face card or a ten. "Twenty-one," the dealer would announce. "That's the name of the game." And men exposing such a hand would assume the deal, placing their chips in the center of the table to be sized up by the man running the game; for the "house" was in on every deal on a fifty-fifty basis.

Gradually Neil comprehended that the object of the game was to get twenty-one or as near to it as possible without getting more than that exact count. He learned that the aces counted eleven, the face cards and ten-spots ten each, and the other cards according to their figures. A face card and seven counted as seventeen. He noticed that the players seldom drew to this count or above it, for they seemed to feel that the chances of getting a four-spot or less were greatly against them. He noticed, too, that when the dealer turned up a twenty-one count on the first two cards he took all bets without permitting any one to draw—except, of course, another twenty-one, which would be a stand-off. But, most important of all, he noted that the best chances for winning lay with the dealer.

As he became more familiar with the play, he felt the fever for gambling burning in his veins. Gambling had been one of his faults in the two tragic years which lay behind him. He had promised Dora never to gamble again; it had virtually been one of the principal provisions of their pact. He wiped huge drops of perspiration from his brow and went to the bar frequently for another drink—forgetting his promise not to touch liquor, too.

When he returned from one of these trips for refreshment he found vacant a seat behind which he had been standing. After hesitating a brief interval he dropped into it, opened his wallet, and flung a twenty-dollar note to the dealer. "All blues," he ordered.

The man in the slot pushed over eight blue chips Neil started. He hadn't watched the buying in of chips closely and had assumed the blue ones were worth a dollar each. He felt he couldn't very well explain, and so he wagered a blue chip as nonchalantly as possible under the circumstances. If he lost them all he could quit. He had had exactly one hundred and ten dollars in his wallet after paying the expenses of the trip and buying the hat.

He lost the first blue chip and then another. He doubled and lost again. He bet the remaining four chips to get even, and the dealer raked in all bets on a black jack—twenty-one.

"How many?" asked the man in the slot cheerfully. The dealer was holding up the deal waiting upon him.

"Twenty again," said Neil, striving to smile as if losing money were nothing to him.

On the last blue chip of the second stack he won the deal with a natural twenty-one hand. But he couldn't take the deal and be prepared to offstand the bets with five dollars in chips which he now had on the table. Nor would the five which the house man would put in with him be enough. Yet the deal offered what was apparently an excellent chance to win.

Neil drew out his wallet and tossed the remainder of his capital to the center of the table. "You handle the cards," he said to the man in the slot, who had done so several times for players.

The deal broke even on the first round of the cards. Neil saw with elation—although not without a subtle sense of misgiving—that the players were making sizable bets. Some wagered the limit of twenty dollars in checks on the second deal. The eighteen count which turned up for the bank on this deal was not sufficient to win all the bets.

"Are you going all the way?" the man in the slot asked Neil.

"Sure," replied Neil, thinking the man meant to ask if he would go for all he had put in the center.

On the third deal a player who had wagered twenty dollars turned a black jack and won immediately on his count of twenty-one. Only two players drew cards, and these announced that they were good. The man dealing turned up a thirteen count. "Come on, eight-spot," he said in coaxing tones, as he turned a card from the top of the pack. A face card fell.

"That breaks us," said the dealer. "Hard luck, but it goes that way sometimes; that's what makes the game. Let's see—we haven't enough chips."

He sized up to all bets around the table. "You owe forty dollars for your half of the overs," he announced to Neil.

Neil paled. "But—but all the money I had on me

was in the center," he explained lamely.

"What's that?" snappily asked the man in the slot. His dark face clouded and his eyes burned. "Didn't you say you'd go all the way? There wasn't enough checks in the center to meet all these bets—you saw that, didn't you?"

"I—I didn't understand what you meant," faltered Neil, the perspiration breaking out upon his forehead anew. "I thought you meant would I—I go for what I had in the center."

"Now, don't come any of that on me," continued the dealer. "Cough up!"

"Just got in with an Eastern bank roll an' wants to make us believe he's broke," jeered a man of tanned visage who wore a rattlesnake-skin band about his wide-brimmed hat and leather cuffs adorned with silver ornaments. "Well, we got a different code out here, stranger. Pay up like a man!"

"But I tell you I haven't any more money," blurted Neil, his face red.

"I'll frisk you," shouted the dealer, starting around the table as the other players leaped back out of the way, "an' if you're broke I'll take it out of your tenderfoot hide, you cheap homesteader."

"Ratty, you shut up an' sit down!" The words came in cool, even tones from behind Neil's chair.

Neil looked up to see a large, red-faced man standing behind him, looking grimly at the dealer, who had halted suddenly.

"You ain't meanin' to say you'd let him get away

with a thing like that, are you, Lentu?" demanded the dealer of the red-faced man.

"Didn't he just tell you he didn't understand what you meant?" demanded Lentu coolly. "Don't you suppose there's any one comes into this country who don't understand blackjack? You sit down, Ratty, and do just what you would have done if he had said he wasn't going all the way. Pay the overs out of the bank."

Ratty slunk back to his place in the slot, trembling with rage.

Neil rose, but his movement was arrested by the sound of another voice, cool and drawling.

"Now, Lent, just because Ratty is goin' to let this cheap skate get away with his four-flush play is not sayin' I'm agreeable." It was the man with the ornamented cuffs—plainly a man of the ranges, for his black, hairy chaps showed as he knocked back his chair and gained his feet.

Neil glimpsed a lightning movement of Lentu's arm at his side; then he gasped. In the flash of an eye his champion had drawn a gun. Held at the hip, its long, black-blue barrel was aimed directly at the heart of the man who had espoused the dealer's cause.

"Out, Ben, out!" said Lentu meaningly, meeting the other's hard gaze unflinchingly. "You're not in the know in this play."

For some moments the two eyed each other steadily. Then the cow-puncher sat down. "All right, Lentu, if that's the way it is," he said simply, and turned his attention again to the table as the other players resumed their chairs.

Lentu put up his gun. "Come along," he said to Neil, and the two left the place.

In the clear, fresh air Neil breathed deeply. This, then, was the West. All the experiences he had had in the past—thrilling as some of them had seemed—were as nothing compared to what he had just gone through. Gun play! Such speed!

From within he heard the sneering, high-pitched voice of Ratty shouting: "A man's hat don't make a man out of a boob."

In that instant there was born in Neil's heart an innate, consuming hatred of the dealer.

## CHAPTER III
### SEEDS OF TRAGEDY

THE man, Lentu, led Neil to a back room in the rear of the New West Hotel bar.

"Bring up a bottle," he instructed the bartender, with a wink, as they passed through to the rear room.

While they were waiting for the order to be executed Lentu regarded Neil thoughtfully. When they had been served and were again alone Lentu spoke:

"Name's Sterret, ain't it?"

Neil nodded wonderingly.

"Old Amos Brodick's nephew from Illinois?"

"Yes," replied Neil readily. "Are you the man sent

by my uncle to take us out to the ranch in the morning?" He had forgotten to make inquiries concerning their escort.

"No; my name's Lentu," explained the other. "But I heard in a sort of roundabout way that you was coming out, heard your name, saw you come in, checked up on the register, and just happened into the Prairie Flower saloon when your trouble started. I'm ready to believe what you said about not understanding what the dealer meant an' all that. Those fellers are layin' for the homesteaders; but you're not a homesteader, of course."

"No, I'm not," affirmed Neil.

"There're a whole lot of things you've got to learn about this country," said Lentu, pouring two more drinks from the bottle and then setting it well aside.

"Yes, yes," agreed Neil eagerly. "I don't know why you have befriended me, but—but I wish I could ask you to teach me to handle a gun like yourself."

Lentu smiled. It was not his part at that time to tell the young man before him that skill of the kind he had exhibited is not easily taught or acquired, that gunmen were more often born than made, and that the practice which perfected them was the natural outgrowth of an early inclination and aptitude.

"I'll do what I can," said Lentil seriously. "But I want to tell you something of conditions hereabouts. Maybe it will all be for your own good. I hope you think I'm in earnest when I say I'm interested in you."

21

"I can see that by the way you acted tonight," said Neil quickly.

Again Lentu smiled; but Neil was toying with his glass and thinking of Ratty, the dealer, and did not see the grim, baffling, designing quality of that smile.

"Sterret," said Lentu earnestly, "this has always been a cattle country. Of late we've had some sheep, but they came in because the homesteaders began to crowd the range. Sheep can graze on less land than cattle—of course, you know that."

Neil did not know it, or had not known it until then, but he inclined his head as if the knowledge had always been his.

"Well, now," continued Lentu, choosing his words carefully and striving to impress his listener as much as possible by the earnestness of his tone, "we could stand a few homesteaders. They gathered in little groups for their own protection"—he paused long enough to wink significantly—"and as long as that was the case we could take care of them easily. But now the government has set up a yell about free land, and the poor fools think all they've got to do is come out here and file, and a farm will sprout.

"Sterret, listen to me." He was in deadly earnest now, and his eyes narrowed as he leaned on the table toward the younger man. "This isn't a farming country. Here and there in the river bottoms we've raised some oats; but on this open range, out on the flat lands away from water, on the benches? Never!"

He struck the table with his fist, and Neil reached forward to steady the lamp.

"These homesteaders," Lentu went on, "inexperienced, land crazy, deluded, are flocking in here to do something that never has been done before—to take away the range that's rightfully ours, to starve our stock and make paupers of us. Do you think that's right, Sterret?"

Neil looked into the grim face before him, into the cool, gray eyes that bored into his own. "I—I don't know much about it," he confessed.

"If a man walked in here, poked a gun in your face, took your watch, and made away with it, would you think it was right?" demanded Lentu.

"Of course not," said Neil hotly. "That would be stealing."

Lentu leaned back. He drew tobacco and papers from his shirt pocket and proceeded to roll a cigarette. "That's what they're doing to us," he said quietly. "They're stealing our range, using the land act as a gun, an' taking the grass away from our cattle. The country has to have cattle, Sterret."

Neil nodded. That fact was indisputable.

"And there are plenty of farming countries where it rains once in a while," Lentu pointed out. "You come from one."

Again Neil nodded. There was logic in what this man said.

Lentu put a light to his cigarette. "Then why," he continued, "should these harebrained homesteaders come out here to steal our range and scatter or kill our herds when there is plenty of farming land elsewhere, and this is a natural stock country?"

Neil could only ponder the question; he could think of no answer. "I don't know," he said finally.

"And nobody else does," declared Lentu. "Listen, Sterret. Your uncle, Amos Brodick, is a cattleman. He always has been a cattleman. The time has come for the cattlemen in the Angel Butte district to stick together. Don't you think he should stick?"

"Why certainly," replied Neil instantly. "He'll stick. Who said he wouldn't stick?"

Lentu merely waved a hand deprecatingly and rose. "I was just acquainting you with the way things stand out here. Thought I'd tell you right off how we are fixed. You're going up to the Brodick ranch and— you'll be a cattleman yourself. We have to understand each other."

Neil felt flattered as he followed Lentu out.

"You better go to your room," advised Lentu. "It's late, anyway, and you ain't very well acquainted out here yet. I'll see you again. Good night."

It was not until Neil had reached the top of the stairs that he recollected he had forgotten to ask Lentu where his ranch was or whom he represented.

He knocked lightly on the door of Dora's room. "You awake?"

"Yes, I was worried about you," replied the girl. "Where have you been?"

"Just looking the town over," he answered.

24

"Is your uncle or his man here to take us to the ranch in the morning?"

"No. I looked everywhere but couldn't find any one; but some one will be here in the morning," he said.

"Neil, are you sure?"

"Yes, there was a man who knows, who said they would. Don't worry."

"Good night, Neil."

For a minute he was silent, and then: "Good night, Dora."

He went to his room, closed and locked the door, and lit the lamp. He laid the new hat on the table, and for a long time sat looking at it, a queer, bright look in his eyes.

"I guess this is the country I've been looking for," he muttered finally.

And long into the night, to the early hours of the morning, he tossed and turned in his bed and stared for extended intervals out of the window at the stars and the velvet black shadows of Angel Butte and the mountains beyond.

In the hotel bar below, Lentu and the cow-puncher Ben were talking.

"So that was who he was," Ben was saying. "An' did you talk some sense into him or did he have some to start with?"

"Well, he's got the makings now, anyway," Lentu said, grinning. "Come on, I've got to go down and square myself with Ratty, or he'll think I'm sidin' with the land grubbers."

"Ratty was plumb puzzled," declared Ben as the two started for the Prairie Flower saloon. "An' you had me goin' for a spell. Amos Brodick's nephew. Lent, you've got more sense than the hull outfit put together!"

"It ain't sense," said Lentu grimly. "It's precaution."

# CHAPTER IV
## SECTION TWENTY-TWO

NEIL and Dora had just finished breakfast in the morning when they were approached by a tall, blond young fellow who swung his dusty, wide-brimmed hat behind him as he inquired: "Is this Mr. Sterret?"

"That's me," said Neil.

"Yore uncle sent me to get you and take you out to the ranch," said the man. "I'm Walt Frost, one of yore uncle's hands."

"This is my wife," said Neil, introducing Dora.

Walt Frost bowed. "Glad to meet you, ma'am. Are you ready to go? I've got the buckboard, an' the horses is rested up; I've been in since five o'clock."

"How is Uncle Brodick?" asked Dora.

"Oh, I plumb went an' forgot to tell you that yore uncle said he was sorry he couldn't get down to meet you, but, you see, we're puttin' the cattle out on the forest range, an' he reckons to keep an' eye on the proceedings. Yore uncle is well, ma'am."

"I guess we're ready to start," said Neil. "You might help me down with the grips."

"Shore I will. You bet," agreed Walt, and he followed Neil upstairs.

When they had carried the baggage to the narrow platform in front of the hotel Walt announced that he would go for the team and asked them to wait a short time.

"Isn't he a nice fellow?" said Dora as they stood on the platform beside their baggage. "Did you notice his laughing blue eyes and how brown his face and hands were—the color of bronze from the sun? Neil, isn't the sun bright out here?"

Neil was about to reply when the hotel clerk touched him lightly on the arm. "About your bill, Mr. Sterret. I thought perhaps you had forgotten," he said politely. "Or perhaps you wish it charged to your uncle's account? All his men stop here when in town."

Neil had grown cold when he heard the first words and remembered that his funds had been exhausted the night before, but he brightened when he heard the clerk's final statement.

"Just put it on uncle's account," he said lightly.

"That's all right, Mr. Sterret. I shouldn't have asked. Was everything satisfactory?"

"No complaint to make," said Neil.

As the clerk stepped back into the hotel Dora spoke. "Oh, Neil, why don't you just pay the bill and not bother uncle about it? I'm sure he'd be better pleased if he knew we hadn't asked any—any favors in getting to the ranch."

"Never mind," said Neil. "We haven't any too much money, and I'm going to work for uncle, am I not?"

"Yes—only I thought—"

"He'll never see it on the bill, anyway," Neil broke in. "They don't look at bills out here; they just pay 'em." He remembered what the cow-puncher in the blackjack game of the night before had said. "Uncle would want us to charge it, anyway."

Dora was silent, thinking.

In another minute Walt Frost drove up in the buckboard, and the hotel runner came hurrying out to help them load their baggage and wish them "good luck" as they sped away behind two splendid bays.

Across the railroad track, past the livery stable and feed corrals and numbers of small shacks and tents, they made their way and eventually emerged upon the prairie which sloped gradually upward in a long acclivity to the shoulders of Angel Butte.

Dora could not repress an exclamation of ecstasy, and Neil, sitting beside her on the rear seat of the buckboard, felt an indescribable thrill as the panorama of a far-flung, wild, lonely, colorful expanse of plain and rolling hills and mountains was unfolded before their eyes.

The vast reaches of level ground, golden under the sun, were splashed with the blooms of prairie cactus; eastward and northward the great, undulating stretches of virgin prairie reached to the blue rim of the horizon; in the northwest the dim, serrated outlines of the mountains hung against the sky and ranged in a hundred-mile semicircle around to the southeast, surmounted at intervals by white peaks, and in the western foreground, toward which they were heading, the pine-clothed sides of Angel Butte sloped down to the grassy flatlands.

"Neil, Neil, did you ever think the world could look so big?" exclaimed Dora, somewhat overawed by the magnificence of the scene.

"It ain't so big but what it's beginning to be crowded, ma'am," said Walt over his shoulder.

Neil remembered the talk of Lentu the night before. "There are strange things happening here, Dora," he said seriously.

"Strange? What do you mean, Neil?"

"I hardly know myself," answered Neil truthfully.

He ignored her further questions as they drove over the smooth prairie road, and soon she forgot to be inquisitive as the grandeur of the view again awoke within her something akin to inspiration and awe.

As the sun ascended in the illimitable blue arch of the heavens they rounded the north shoulder of Angel Butte and began a long ascent.

Suddenly, from around a bend above, two horsemen came into view, riding furiously. Walt gave vent to a startled exclamation and pointed excitedly. Almost immediately another rider could be seen, urging his mount at breakneck speed in pursuit of the pair ahead.

White puffs of smoke broke from in front of the third horseman.

Walt pulled up the team just as the flying pair reached the buckboard. Before there was time for explanations or questioning the third rider reached them.

Neil recognized Lentu. He waved to him, but Lentu paid no attention to them. Instead he addressed himself to the two who had halted when they had come up to the team. "What were you doing up on the north half of twenty-two?" he demanded crisply.

"The north half of that section isn't filed on, is it?" asked one of the men.

"If you mean that it's still open on the maps I reckon you're right," replied Lentu, holding his gun in view.

"Well—we—we supposed if it was still open on the maps, it was opened to filing," explained the first man, visibly nervous.

Lentu urged his horse close beside the speaker's. He looked the man square in the eye; fixed him with a narrowed, dangerous gaze. "It's open on the maps and open to filin', but it's across the line," he said steadily.

"Line? What line?"

"Suppose you ask 'em down at Angel," replied Lentu. "An' when you find out what I mean maybe you'll be more careful in the matter of judgment." He tapped the horn of his saddle with the barrel of his gun. "Understand," he continued in the same cool, ominous voice, "it's open on the maps, an' it's open to filing, only—it's across the line. So long."

The two men, evidently from some other part of the country, swung their horses about, after a few seconds of indecision, and rode away.

Lentu turned to the occupants of the buckboard. "Howdy, Walt! Hello there, Sterret!" he greeted.

Walter merely nodded curtly. Sterret returned the greeting verbally and, after Lentu had replied with a formal remark about the weather, introduced Dora.

"A pleasure, Mrs. Sterret," said Lentu, swinging low his hat. "An' now, if you folks don't mind my breaking trail for you, I'll be back on my way."

He whirled his horse and was gone in a cloud of dust.

"You know him?" asked Walt of Neil before he started the horses.

"Met him last night," answered Neil. "Say, Walt, who is he?"

"That's Lentu," said Walt quietly.

"I know his name; but what about him?"

"He's foreman for the Double S."

Dora, who had crouched against Neil at sight of the gun, now recovered herself. "But why was he chasing those men and—and firing at them?" she asked. "And what did he mean by the north half of twenty-two?"

"We'll be at the ranch in an hour," was Walt's cryptic reply.

# CHAPTER V
## AMOS BRODICK

SHORTLY after noon they crossed the west shoulder of Angel Butte, where it was joined by a spur from the mountains, and looked down into a beautiful valley between pine-clothed hills, through which wound a stream of clear water called Wild Horse Creek.

Walt pointed with his whip to the lower end of the valley, south of the butte, where a set of substantial ranch buildings showed the center of tilled fields looking like green squares of velvet with silver bands, where the irrigation ditches gleamed in the bright sunlight of midday.

"The ranch," he said proudly; "the 3-X-Z."

On the lower slopes of the hills cattle were feeding, and a band of horses was grazing along the creek bottom upstream from the ranch. South and west the green ranges rose in long steps, studded with virgin stands of pine and fir, to the white peaks which reared against the sky.

Again Dora and Neil stared in wonder, silenced by the glory and stupendous beauty of the scene. It was as if they had stepped from the plain into the mountains. And then the panorama was shut off as they drove down into a wide cañon, its sides covered with firs, and began the descent to Wild Horse Creek.

Dora gasped and squealed with fright as the buckboard rattled along the narrow road with less than a foot to spare between the edge of the road and the precipitous side of the cañon.

Soon, however, they came out upon a better road in Wild Horse Valley and drove swiftly down along the stream. Walt stopped the team, got out with a large drinking cup, and handed them each a drink of the clear, cold water.

"It's the best water I ever drank!" said Dora, asking for more.

"Yes, it's tolerably fair water, ma'am," agreed Walt. "This creek is fed by mountain springs. But wait until you drink some of the spring water at the ranch. Yore uncle had it piped from some springs about a mile up the creek on the south side, an' it's supposed to be the best water hereabouts."

Half a mile farther they reached the upper end of the ranch and then rode between green fields and pastures. At last they turned in between two high gateposts, while a boy held the gate open lest it swing back, and drove up to the vine-covered side porch of the ranch house.

A woman, Amos Brodick's capable housekeeper, welcomed them.

"Mr. and Mrs. Sterret!" she exclaimed, visibly excited and delighted. "So you're here 'way back from Illinoy. I declare you must be tired. I'm Mrs. French, your uncle's housekeeper. Come right in. Louis, Louis! Come here and help with their things. That's my boy," she explained as a freckled, brown-haired lad came bashfully forward.

"He's a little backward with strangers," went on Mrs. French while she led them into the first room off the porch, which proved to be the dining room. "Expect you'll want to tidy up a bit. Right this way, Mrs. Sterret, dear. Louis, you show Mr. Sterret where to wash. I declare you must be starved. Now just fix yourself up a bit, Mrs. Sterret, and I'll have your dinner ready in a jiffy."

Ten minutes later they sat down to a dinner of roast beef, mashed potatoes, thick gravy, pickles, creamed corn, jellies, cold tomato sauce, biscuits, honey, raisin pie and jelly tarts—all served with pitchers of rich milk and cups of steaming coffee.

"Your uncle is up the creek putting the beef herd on the forest reserve range," said Mrs. French, hovering about them as they ate. "He'll be back for supper, an' he'll sure be glad to see you all. Now don't be backward 'bout helping yourselves; we eat all we want out here and ain't ashamed of it. Dear me, I declare I'm glad to have a woman to talk to on this ranch, Mrs. Sterret."

"Won't you just call me Dora?" asked the girl, who already had taken a great liking to the housekeeper.

"Well, just listen to that!" blustered Mrs. French, very much delighted. "Of course I will, dear—Dora it is. I declare I'm glad you are regular folks. I was afraid you might be a little high-toned, coming from the East that a way."

"Neil, perhaps Mrs. French can tell us why the men

were shooting over there when we came up," said Dora, again remembering the shots and the strange actions of the men they had met.

"Oh, it must be Martin's doings," said Mrs. French quickly. "They are trying to stop the homesteaders from locating around the butte. Was it anything to frighten you, dear? I'm so sorry."

"But is it right for them to shoot at men, Mrs. French?"

"No, deary, it isn't." Mrs. French looked worried for a second. "But your uncle will tell you about it, or I will later. And it's nothing for us to worry over."

"When will Uncle Amos be back?" asked Neil.

"Late this afternoon. He has to help the men. We are short-handed now because it's hard to get men for a cattle ranch."

"I should think the homesteaders would be looking for jobs," said Neil.

"Some of them will work, Mr. Sterret, but they're inexperienced. We've only got about twelve men now, not counting the cook."

"Can't uncle get all the men he wants?" persisted Neil.

Mrs. French made a gesture of helplessness. "It doesn't seem that way," she confessed. "Things are none too good lately."

"None too good? What do you mean by that?"

"Well, Mr. Sterret, you better wait and talk with your uncle. He can tell you more than I can," said Mrs. French as she began to clear the table.

Dora offered to help, and Neil went out to look over the ranch. Louis accompanied him and showed him the bunk house where the men slept and kept their belongings, the cook house and men's dining room, adjoining the bunk house; then they went to view the barns and corrals, and Louis took him to the stream behind the hay barn, where they caught a mess of trout.

Just before sundown Amos Brodick and several other men came riding furiously down the valley and swung in to the barns amid a cloud of dust.

Ten minutes later Amos Brodick was greeting his nephew.

"Mighty glad you took it into your head to come out to this country," he boomed cheerfully in a hearty greeting as he gripped Neil's hand. "An' now, Neil, where's your wife?"

Dora came out upon the porch when Neil called and offered her hand a bit timidly to the big man who was to play such an important part in their destinies.

"Waal, now, Neil, you sure picked a good looker," declared Amos. "That ain't flattery, young lady; we tell people what we think of 'em out here as often as not. Now let's all go in an' get supper. I'm hungry enough to eat ground hog tonight—if we didn't have anything else."

After supper Neil and his uncle sat on the porch, where they could see the high light in the western skies and the white gleam of the limestone cliffs against the dark green of the pine growth on the hills.

Dora, who had been talking with them, had gone into the house and again was busy helping Mrs. French.

"That's a queer story Dora and you have told me," said Amos Brodick. "But I guess the little girl has the right ideer. You know, Neil, a man's got to have a woman's respect to be the right sort of husband, an' this is a country which makes men—or starts 'em on the road to making themselves."

Neil avoided further talk about his and Dora's affairs. "What's this I hear from Lentu about the trouble the homesteaders are making out here?" he asked.

Amos Brodick frowned. "It wouldn't be my ideer, exactly, to have you worrying your head about our troubles the first day you get here," he said. "But one reason I was glad when you decided to come was because I kinda need the help of some one of my own blood. I'm all alone here, and I ain't always sure who to trust."

"I understand you are finding it hard to get men," prompted Neil.

"Yes, and that's a bit strange, too," said Amos. "Of course there ain't as many men in this country now who know this business, the cattle business. But the dry-landers, as we call 'em, who are filin' on the land, seem scared to come out Angel Butte way to work. I think Lentu an' his crowd have got 'em buffaloed."

"What's Lentu got to do with it?"

"Lentu is foreman for Martin, who owns the Double

S. Martin and McCabe, of the T-C, and Pierson, of the old Angel Butte Cattle Company's ranch, the A B C, have gotten together with the ideer of fightin' the homesteaders. The Double S, T-C, A B C, and myself own quite a piece of land in here; enough so we can run quite a bunch of cattle, although not as many as up to a year ago.

"This combine, as I call the Angel Butte crowd, aims to keep ranging cattle north and east of the butte by intimidating the men who've filed on land there—by gun play, if necessary. They've made the north half of section twenty-two an outlaw piece by scarin' off people who've come up there to file on it; say that's as far south as locatin' can be done. An' it's wrong, to my notion."

"Aren't you with the combine, Uncle Amos?" asked Neil.

"Not in that way," replied the older man quickly. "I ain't aiming to try to fight the government, for that's what it amounts to. We had the free use of this land for grazing, but it never belonged to us. We've grabbed off a chunk as it is. Now, if the government wants to come in and say we're goin' to give away that land, why, it's the government's right. I can make out pretty well by breeding better stock—goin' in for quality more'n quantity—an' the combine can do the same."

"But won't the combine look at it as if you wasn't sticking by the stock interests?" demanded Neil.

Amos Brodick turned and regarded his nephew in the half light. "I can see you've been thinking a lot about what Lentu has been telling you," he said earnestly. "Now don't go too much by what he says. Your interests are here with me, for now that you're out here I don't mind telling you that I figure on teaching you how to run this ranch and on leaving it to you when I die. Don't think too one-sided, one way or the other; but think fair."

Two horsemen came riding down the valley road, and one of them turned in at the gate and spurred his horse up the road to the porch.

"Hello there, Swain," called Amos. "Get down here a minute; I want you to meet my nephew, Neil Sterret, son of my sister's. He just got in from the East. Neil, this is Swain, my foreman."

When the two men had shaken hands Amos and Swain spoke about range matters for a few minutes. "We've been putting the beef herd on forest-reserve range today," explained Amos to Neil as the foreman vaulted into the saddle to take his horse to the barn.

"By the way," said Swain after he had mounted. "I met a hombre riding slow this way leading a pack horse. Stranger hereabouts, I guess. Asked him if he wanted a job, an' he said he couldn't make up his mind."

"What kind of a lookin' feller?" asked Amos.

"Tall, dark, clean-shaven," replied Swain. "Sat his horse like he was used to saddle leather an' had a gun slung handy. Seemed a cheerful sort of cuss with a don't-give-a-darn air about him as if he was plumb sure he could take care of himself. I don't know—

there was something in the way he sat, or held his arm, or— Oh, I don't know what, but he looked to me—"

"Swain, what're you gettin' at?" demanded Amos impatiently.

"Well, he impressed me the first crack out of the box as being a gunman, maybe," explained Swain as he rode away. "He might likely be down this way," the foreman called back over his shoulder.

"I'd like to have a look at him," mused Amos Brodick as they turned into the house. "I wonder if it could be anybody I know."

# CHAPTER VI
## THE STRANGER

WHEN Neil came down from his room at dawn the following morning he was surprised to find that the others, including Dora, were all up and about. After breakfast Amos Brodick took him out to the barn, where he showed him a rangy sorrel in a box stall.

"That's your horse, Neil," said Amos, "an' I guess about the first thing you better do is to get used to a saddle. Walt'll show you some saddles, an' you can pick out the one that suits you best."

Neil explained that he had done quite a bit of riding on the farm in the East, and his uncle nodded approvingly. "You'll have to be on a horse a good bit of the time out here," he told Neil, "an' the main thing is to get over the soreness soon's you can."

Dora, too, was given a mount, and that afternoon, when Neil and Walt had ridden up the valley to look after some stock grazing in the bottoms above the ranch, she rode along the trail which led north up a long draw toward the east shoulder of Angel Butte.

Lured on by the beauty which revealed itself in the vistas of pine-rimmed stream and picturesque cliffs, she rode farther than she had intended, and suddenly she realized that she was tired and stiff in the saddle.

She dismounted to rest in a little mountain park near the head of the draw, where the sides of the hills on either hand crowded in against the narrow trickle of stream and trail. She tied her horse to an aspen and reclined against the soft bed of grass and moss. The sides of the draw were thick with chokecherry bushes, while in the open spaces among the timbers higher up grew the low, gray vines of the cedar, or juniper, berries. Wild roses and other mountain flowers were scattered about in profusion, and the breeze was sweet with the scent of blossoms and the resinous tang of the timber.

The peaceful beauty of the scene and the stillness of this region so new and strange to her impressed her with a sense of quiet and repose. With eyes half closed she began to dream of a new life in which Neil would find himself, and happiness would come to them both.

Soon she was dozing, and then she slept, falling a victim to the seductive powers of sun and breeze and the altitude of the hills which so often affect people unaccustomed to them in this combination.

She was awakened by the pound of hoofs and opened her eyes with a startled cry to see Neil dismounting before her.

"They told me you'd come up this way, and I followed you, thinking you might get lost," he explained as he threw the reins over his horse's head with a motion he already had learned.

"I rode farther than I intended and got off to rest," said Dora sheepishly, as she fixed her hair and rose to her feet.

Neil stepped toward her. "Dora, you look positively adorable," he said in unsullied admiration. "You look sweet enough to kiss."

She drew back from him. "Now you're forgetting your promise," she reminded him.

"But, Dora, can't a man praise his wife?" he demanded.

"I suppose so," she said doubtfully, her face flushed. "But is that all you mean, Neil—just praise?"

"No, it isn't," he replied earnestly and truthfully. "Dora, we can't go on this way for a whole year. I realized it today. I need you to help me make good. And, as it is now, people will wonder; they will laugh at us behind our backs. Didn't you see the queer look on Uncle Amos' face last night when we were talking about how—how it was we came out here? Dora, I never could stand being ridiculed."

"Neil, no one who knows will ridicule us, and they

will have all the more friendly interest in you. Why, Mrs. French said it would prove the best thing in the world for you—"

"Oh, hang Mrs. French!" shouted Neil. "So you've been telling her everything, and soon the whole ranch will know."

"But I had to tell Mrs. French, Neil. And suppose the whole ranch does know—"

"I tell you I can't stand it," he interrupted. "It's all foolishness. And you know it's all different in this country; a man's wife is his wife out here!"

"Let's go back," said Dora hurriedly, starting for her horse.

"Not until I've kissed you and had a better understanding about things," he exclaimed, leaping to her side.

"Neil!" She screamed as he seized her in his arms.

When he kissed her she screamed again and struggled to release herself.

From the slope behind them came the rattle of falling rocks and gravel; then a cool, ominous, drawling voice:

"Turn that girl loose!"

Neil released his hold and whirled to confront a tall, dark man who wore a gun low on his right thigh.

Dora, flushed and panting, with eyes flashing fire, could not resist a grateful glance toward the newcomer.

"What business is it of yours?" demanded Neil angrily.

"Just this much," retorted the man, striding toward him, "your presence and actions don't appear pleasing to the young lady, an' that's enough to excuse my butting in."

"I want you to know that this girl is my—"

"Never mind what you want me to know," interrupted the stranger coolly. "I already know what I've seen with my own eyes. Suppose you beat it out of here—pronto."

"You've got a lot of nerve," blurted Neil, with baffled rage blazing from his eyes.

In a flash the stranger's gun leaped into his hand. "You goin' to obey orders an' lope?" he demanded ominously.

"I'm not going to go without—"

"Wait," cried Dora. "I'll go first." She untied her horse and, leading him to a rock, used the boulder as an aid in mounting. "You can follow me, Neil," she called back.

Neil climbed into his saddle. "I haven't got any gun," he said with a sneer as he gave the sorrel the rein.

"Maybe it's a good thing you haven't," said the stranger, putting away his own weapon.

When Neil had gone the man climbed quickly to a point where a horse stood on a thin ribbon of trail. "Lucky for the girl I happened to be scouting down this way," he muttered to himself. Then he laughed. "No gun!"

He turned his horse up the mountain toward the

summit of Angel Butte. But as he rode he twisted frequently in the saddle to survey the country.

# CHAPTER VII
## GOSPEL OF THE RANGE

EARLY next morning the newcomer in the Angel Butte section rode slowly down the north slope of the butte and from a point of vantage scanned the open country to the north and east. He sat his horse quietly, rolled and lit innumerable cigarettes, tipped his hat to shade his eyes from the bright sun, and evidently enjoyed the lonesome panorama of wild, open distances spread out before him.

Despite his apparent calmness there was about him a subtle attitude of impatience; his eyes, alert and keen, roved constantly over the scene and frequently searched the timbered areas behind him. Occasionally he twisted and turned in his saddle and spoke vaguely to his horse—a perfect specimen of the enduring Western cow pony.

His attention became focused upon two riders who were making their way slowly up the long, grassy acclivity toward the western shoulder of the butte.

And suddenly he started and uttered an exclamation of surprise as he noted spurts of dust in the road just ahead of the riders, who now halted instantly.

"Bullets!" he cried in amazement.

He whirled his horse about and spurred along a

45

cross-cut toward the two men sitting their mounts in indecision.

Rounding a rise of ground he whistled as he descried two other mounted men speeding from the west side of the butte toward the motionless riders.

"Now what kind of a game is this?" he asked aloud as he urged his horse at a tangent toward the place where the men were likely to meet.

When he reached the spot the four were engaged in what appeared to be a one-sided conversation. The quartet regarded him questioningly as he rode up and reined in his horse.

"Well?" snapped one of the men who wore chaps and spurs and was armed with a six-gun and had a carbine slung in its sheath from his saddle horn.

"Nice day," said the stranger casually.

"Just right for ridin'; don't let us delay you none," said another of the men, dressed and armed like the first speaker.

The other two men were attired more after the manner of the towns and were not armed. They plainly were flustered.

"I was wondering what it was all about," said the stranger pointedly.

"It don't concern you onless yore a dirty, lowdown homesteader," said the first man, whirling his horse to confront the stranger.

The stranger smiled. "An' if I am a homesteader?" he suggested.

"Then yo're on dangerous ground," snappily replied

the other. "This pair has just found out where they stand," he continued, indicating the two men who were not armed.

"We're homesteaders," confessed one of the men, "and we understood the north half of section twenty-two was open to entry, also some land south of it, and we came up to see it."

"An' you can go back an' tell the locator that told you about it that the next time a party comes up here we're goin' to shoot to hit something beside the grass roots," shouted the spokesman for the armed pair.

"That's mighty rough language, friend," observed the stranger.

"We don't aim to decorate the truth up in no parlor style," retorted the other.

The stranger's right hand hovered stiffly above the black butt of the gun at his right side, and he regarded the speaker with an unwavering gaze as he spoke to the homesteaders.

"You seen this land you're talking about?" he asked quietly.

The homesteaders at first did not realize he was speaking to them. Finally one of them answered: "If you mean us—yes, we've seen it."

"And you're sure it's open to entry?" continued the stranger.

"Yes, it's open—and a good piece, too."

"Then why don't you go ahead and file!" said the stranger crisply as the gun leaped to his hand ahead of the concerted attempt of the two armed men to draw.

"You fellows don't hardly figure you're bigger than Uncle Sam, do you?" he demanded of the pair who had gone motionless when his gun had appeared.

"Yo're a stranger in these parts, ain't you?" sneeringly asked one of the men.

"Sure," replied the stranger. "But I get at home quick when there's gun play goin' on."

The homesteaders, visibly relieved and with revived confidence, turned their horses and rode away in the direction of the town, miles eastward.

And the two men confronting the stranger also turned their mounts—westward. "I've got you spotted," said the spokesman in a tone which meant much. "Yo're Brodick's gunman!"

But the stranger merely laughed—a merry, tantalizing laugh—as the pair dashed away. Then he rode slowly back toward the east side of the butte, whistling as though his mood had changed; as though something he had craved had taken place to disrupt the monotony of the peaceful scene before him. And in his gray eyes was a leaping fire of excitement, evidently relished.

The two men who had intimidated the homesteaders rode at a furious pace up the road and turned in at a stone ranch house near the pass over the west shoulder of the butte.

Dashing up to the house they dismounted, flung the reins over their horses' heads, went to the door, and knocked. Almost instantly the door was opened, and the men walked into what was plainly an office room.

Lentu, who had opened the door, greeted them gruffly. A large, gray-haired man with a florid face and bushy eyebrows sat at a desk.

"What's up?" he demanded. "I thought you were guarding twenty-two."

"So we was," explained one of the men. "But a new hand's been taken in the game."

"New hand?" queried the man at the desk. "Come, talk up."

"Well, I guess as owner of the Double S you'll be surprised to learn that the homesteaders has got a new ally," said the man, reveling in the element of suspense he was creating.

"Out with it," snapped Lentu, glancing significantly at his employer.

The man then told of the meeting with the homesteaders and the stranger.

"It must be the man we saw riding down the Timber Creek trail night afore last when we was keeping an eye on old man Brodick's movements," concluded Will Martin, owner of the Double S.

"Describe him again, an' don't overlook anything," said Lentu eagerly, his eyes glowing.

Once again the men described the man who had interrupted their play with the two homesteaders.

Lentu swore. "I wonder who it could be. It's a gospel of the range that a gun-fightin' ex-cowman won't even associate with a dry-lander."

"I'll tell you what I think," said the spokesman for the two men who had brought the news. "He came from around the east side of the butte; you people saw him ridin' down Timber Creek the day old Brodick put his beef herd on the forest range; I'll bet he's Brodick's gunman!"

"I've always figured he'd try a trick like that," cried Martin, striking the desk with his fist. "Lentu, this thing is coming to a show-down!"

Lentu sat upon a chair near the desk. He motioned to the two men standing. "Go back and keep an eye out. Send some one to the top of the butte with a glass an' tell him to watch the east side. Florry's around with nothing to do—send him."

When the men had departed he turned to Martin. "You're dead right," he said earnestly. "I'd liked to had a chance to put another bee or two in that fool Sterret's ear, but it looks as if we'd have to go ahead."

Martin shifted uneasily. "I ain't positive, Lentu, that we're on the right track in this business with old Brodick—"

"You ain't goin' to let him cut loose an' fight us in the bargain, are you?" interrupted Lentu.

"No, no," said Martin, avoiding the other's gaze. Then his eyes blazed. "It's up to him to stick!" he exclaimed.

"Sure—sure it is," agreed Lentu in a purring voice, "and as long as we're going through with this thing we might as well go all the way. If Brodick has hired a gunman—" He tapped the butt of his six-shooter significantly.

"I know," said Martin, upon whom the movement

was not lost. "You're fast, Lentu; you're powerful fast. That's one reason I've hung on to you through thick an' thin. You'd been strung up once if I hadn't come to the front for you."

"An' now you're drawing down the interest in full," said Lentu. "I'll send the word to the T-C and the A B C."

Again Martin shifted as though he were ill at ease.

"You think—it's your idea then—so soon?" he faltered.

"Tonight!" said Lentu, rising.

A few minutes afterward riders were pounding toward the T-C ranch in the west and the A B C in the southwest ten miles.

At sunset a number of mounted men were at the Double S. Their horses fed in the corrals while they ate and talked in the ranch house. It was dark when the cavalcade filed into the road that led over the west shoulder of the butte and down the cañons to Timber Creek and the Brodick ranch.

And while they walked their horses under the pale glow of the stars a man cut down through the timber on the south side of the butte and waited in the shadows near the Timber Creek trail.

# CHAPTER VIII
## AN ULTIMATUM

DORA sat at her window. The ranch house was still, and the only sound to be heard was the occasional stamping of the horses in the pasture inclosure across the road. The fields and the timbered sides of the hills were bathed in silvery moonlight, and the limestone rimrock, which traced a series of broad steps up the slope of Angel Butte in the north, was ghostly white.

More and more Dora was impressed by the silence and majesty and overwhelming bigness of this new country. But there were tears in her eyes. Would Neil respond to the wholesome influence of this great outdoors? Had she made a mistake? Was the man she would make over past the point where environment would affect him?

His increasing disposition toward an intolerance of their relations worried her. His outburst of two days before remained fresh in her mind; as did the picture of the tall, dark man with the gray eyes who had come so unexpectedly to her rescue.

And Neil's declaration: "A man's wife is his wife out here!" Was she being selfish?

Deep down in her heart she knew she loved this prodigal. She had loved him when she had promised his mother to marry him. And she suddenly realized that if he failed to make himself the man she wanted for her true husband it would break her heart.

As she gave free rein to these troublesome thoughts and pondered her problem she became conscious of a new sound—a muffled, baffling, indefinable sound. It seemed to come from the west, from the direction of the trail up Timber Creek.

She leaned out of the window, tipping back the screen to do so, and soon caught sight of a number of dark shadows in the road which wound down along the creek. Nearly breathless with interest she watched until the shadows solidified into horses and men. They rode to the gate and there dismounted while one of their number proceeded to the house and knocked upon the door.

In a few seconds she heard some one stirring downstairs. A shaft of yellow light slanted across the grass beneath, as the door swung back and she heard Amos Brodick's voice.

"Howdy, Martin. You're visitin' kinda late, ain't you? Come in."

"No, I don't think I'll come in, Amos, thanks," replied Martin. "Some of the boys are here with me."

"I was wonderin' who was out there by the gate," said Amos, advancing upon the porch with the lamp. "What's the cause for the crowd, Martin?"

"No harm in a crowd, Amos, when you don't know what to expect," was Martin's rejoinder.

"An' what're you meanin' by that?" Amos demanded, surprised.

"We want to talk to you privatelike," explained

Martin steadily. "McCabe an' Pierson are out there, an' some of the men off my place an' the T-C and the A B C ranches. We want to have a conference with you."

"Well, what's the matter with my house?" asked Amos sternly.

"There's no use waking everybody up, Amos; suppose we go out by the corrals."

"This looks to me like a danged dark way of doing business, Martin. I want to ask you again what the idea was in bringing so many men if you just wanted to talk with me, an' why you didn't come in the daytime since you all claim to be honest men."

"We came in a hurry," Martin retorted sharply. "Only McCabe, Pierson, Lentu, an' myself want to talk to you. I'll call 'em in if you aim you've got to have it that way, but there ain't no sense in wakin' the house up an' having 'em all wonderin' an' askin' questions."

"Maybe you're right, but it looks queer to me," Amos said, after deliberating. "But wait till I put this lamp in, an' I'll go out an' hear what you've got to say."

Dora heard Amos Brodick go back into the house. The shaft of yellow light was blotted out. In another minute Amos had joined the man Martin before the house, and the two of them were walking toward the corrals. She saw the man with her uncle raise a hand and saw three others from the horsemen by the gate join them. They disappeared around the corner of the horse barn, and again the night was still.

Though she could not, in her excitement and bewilderment, form a dependable idea of the nature of the mission of Martin and the others of the mounted men, she surmised that in some way an attempt was being made to intimidate Amos Brodick. And while she could not know it, her surmise was not far from the truth.

"Look here, Brodick, this thing has come to a showdown," exclaimed McCabe, owner of the T-C, when the five men had reached the west side of the barn, which was farthest from the bunk house.

"That suits me," replied Amos Brodick instantly. "Lay your cards down."

"Are you in with us to keep this end of the range tight?" demanded McCabe.

"What do you mean by 'keeping it tight?'"

"Keeping the rats out of it!" said Lentu, speaking as if he snarled the words.

McCabe silenced the Double S foreman. "Let me talk," he snapped; then, turning to Amos Brodick: "We mean to keep it tight by keeping these land-grabbing fool homesteaders an' all others with bunch grass for brains off it," he said evenly. "Listen, Brodick, the time's come to throw a good live scare into that bunch an' make 'em lay off the Angel Butte country forever!"

"If that's the play, men, I don't want a hand," said Amos Brodick. "I've got enough to 'tend to without going in for a range war. I've been in one o' them, ain't I, Martin?"

"Don't throw *that* up at me," said Martin with a side glance at Lentu.

"I'm not throwing up anything against you, Martin," said Amos sharply. "Bygones is bygones with me—so far's that's concerned. But I'm not going into a losing game when I can see the handwritin' against it on every plot the land offices are handin' out."

"Amos, if you ever mention the Sand Creek hangin' business again, I swear I'll kill you," said Martin. "I'll—"

"Shut up!" said Lentu.

"I wasn't intendin' to mention the Sand Creek hanging," said Amos dryly; "but now that you've brought it up I can point to it as one reason why you an' me couldn't go into the same deal on any proposition."

"Wait a minute," ordered McCabe. "Here, Brodick, this isn't a personal quarrel. Bad blood between you an' Martin has got nothing to do with this business we're talking about—making the Angel Butte range tight. Now, Brodick, you're a cattleman. We're cattlemen. We own quite a bit of land hereabouts, an' we own lots of stock. We've got to put a stop to this homestead business or we won't have the range for our stock. The forest reserve is a joke, an' you know it. We've got to stick together. Either you're for us or you're against us!"

"Now that ain't exactly fair, McCabe, an' well you know it," replied Amos.

"We're gettin' right down to cases on this proposition," said McCabe. "Martin an' Pierson an' I are in to stick. We've run our stock together for more'n twenty years, an' you've done the same. It's your place to stick with us. That's it—you're either for us or you're against us."

"It looks to me, boys, like there was more behind this thing than just keepin' the homesteaders off like you say," drawled Amos.

For a moment there was silence.

"What's your answer?" demanded McCabe.

"You boys knew before you came down here that I wouldn't agree to no war against the homesteaders," continued Amos in his drawl, which was a danger sign.

"What do you say?" roared Martin.

"It looks pretty much to me like there was something sort of personal in all this business," said Amos.

McCabe motioned to Martin to be silent as the other started to reply. "You can look at it any way you choose," he said to Amos, "but we're askin' you for the last time if you're goin' to stick with us. We'll never ask you again."

"That's a threat!" cried Amos. "An' no man livin' can threaten me into anything. Get out of here!"

"We'll take that for your answer," said Pierson quickly, speaking for the first time.

"An' don't forget who said it," warned Amos Brodick as the four men turned to go.

Dora, still watching from her window, saw the men reappear. Her uncle walked alone toward the house, but directly in front of the porch steps he stopped and, standing in the full light of the moon, watched the men as they mounted their horses at the gate and rode rapidly away up the valley.

Amos Brodick walked slowly down the walk toward the gate, looking after the disappearing horsemen, apparently thinking. As he reached the gate a figure darted from the screen of a clump of pines in the pasture across the road, vaulted the fence, and hurried to the gate.

The girl caught a dull gleam of metal in her uncle's hand as he challenged the newcomer, but the gleam vanished when the lone visitor laughed and said in a rich, musical voice: "Just dropped in to get acquainted, Brodick. I see you been receiving callers."

"An' who are you?" demanded Amos.

The other removed his hat and spoke a few words in an undertone, leaning close to Amos Brodick's ear. Dora started in surprise as she recognized her champion of the incident with Neil in the cañon on the east slopes of Angel Butte.

"Come in," she heard Amos Brodick saying.

The two men entered the house, and Dora crept wonderingly to bed.

# CHAPTER IX
## THE UNFINISHED SENTENCE

I N the first flush of dawn the stranger rode up the cañon trail to the west shoulder of Angel Butte. He saw three men before the main gate to the Double S ranch; two of the men were sitting their horses in the road, and the third was standing by the gate with his shoulders against the crossbars.

As the stranger approached, lounging in the saddle, he drew the attention of all three. Noting this fact, he began to whistle a vagrant tune of the ranges; also he pulled the broad brim of his black, high-crowned hat well forward to shade his eyes from the bright rays of the early morning sun.

"Howdy," greeted Martin of the Double S, scowling as he stepped a bit forward from his position by the gate when the lone rider came up.

"Howdy," returned the stranger without checking his horse.

McCabe, master of the T-C, pushed his horse casually into the path of the newcomer. "Ain't you goin' to stop a minute?" he asked.

The stranger pulled up his horse and favored the speaker with a searching glance. "I've got plenty of time," he drawled. "Was you wanting to ask me, maybe, about something?"

A ranch hand came running from the direction of the house. He made a sign to Martin, who then waved him back.

"I reckon you're out takin' the mornin' air," observed Martin, a gleam of anger in his eyes.

The stranger whirled his horse in Martin's direction so suddenly that the rancher leaped back against the gate. And now the stranger's eyes gleamed with a grim ferocity as he leaned over the saddle horn toward Martin.

"What's the use beatin' around the bush?" he demanded.

McCabe and the other rider closed in a bit, scenting an emergency; their hands dropped toward their pistol butts.

Martin, momentarily taken aback, rallied with flashing eyes at this show of support from McCabe and the ranch hand with him. Though Martin was unarmed he did not fail to discern the angle at which the stranger hooked his right arm above the gun at his side.

"You're a good guesser," said Martin. "Maybe you was just wantin' to know about the road to Angel. The road you're on will take you to town if—"

The stranger laughed harshly. "Martin, I can find my way to a town by instinct. I'm that smart, understand."

"Maybe your friends that was figurin' on filin' on twenty-two is in there waitin' for you!" roared Martin in quick anger.

"Oh! That's it," said the stranger in a soft, musical voice. "You heard about that, eh? Well, now, that land's open to entry, ain't it—or, isn't it? You know I

60

ain't right smart in everything, Martin; maybe that land's yours, now."

Martin, who had been startled to hear the man call him by name, motioned to McCabe to be silent. To all outward appearances the baron of the Double S now was cool. "You're a cow-puncher?" he asked in more agreeable tones.

"I have punched cows."

"Are you lookin' for a job?" asked Martin pleasantly.

"That would depend on who was offering it to me," replied the other coolly.

"I might be able to use a man on the Double S," said Martin.

"Why, you sure ain't gettin' short of guards for that twenty-two tract already!" exclaimed the stranger in mock surprise.

"No, we're not gettin' short," cried Martin, once more burning with anger.

"Wait a minute, Bill," McCabe put in. "Let me ask this feller a few questions—"

"No, let me answer 'em before you ask 'em," the stranger cut in evenly, shifting his keen gaze back and forth between the two ranch owners. "I ain't lookin' for a job, an' I ain't telling you who I am or what I am—I'm that independent," he went on. "It's none o' your business. Maybe I'm just passing through, an' maybe I'll elect to stay aroun' here a while. Maybe I like to fish, an' the fishing's good in the creeks hereabouts. Maybe I'm goin' in for homesteadin', an' maybe I was just attracted to that little fracas over on twenty-two because I like to see fair play. That's some more of my business. I've got all kinds of business; you wouldn't think I had so much business; I'm just chock-full of it. An' it's none o' yours. That's the main point—it's none o' yours. You're wantin' to warn me to get away from Angel Butte. This is a free country, an' I'm over twenty-one. I've camped on the east side of the butte, an' that's on forest reserve. I don't like people aroun' close, maybe; it's just possible I don't like to be crowded. It's likely I don't reckon on being bothered. You was goin' to warn me, and I'll beat you to it—don't you bother me!"

A glance, rich with significance, flashed between McCabe and Martin. "Nice morning," said McCabe with a sneer.

"An' so far it's been a healthy one," rejoined the stranger as he turned his horse back into the road.

"Was there anything you overlooked saying?" asked McCabe with mock politeness.

"I think I was intending to include the intelligence that you men could go to blazes so far's I was concerned if you behaved proper," drawled the stranger, grinning. "But we'll let it go since I forgot it."

Gently he put the spurs to his horse, but as he moved off his eyes sought Martin's and narrowed. "How do you stack up as a guesser?" was his parting shot.

He rode leaning far to the left in his saddle and glancing back over his right shoulder.

"Told us more'n he thought," was McCabe's comment.

Martin nodded silently. "Brodick's hired a gunman," he said.

Shortly after the stranger had passed from sight around the north side of the butte, McCabe and his man took their departure.

The last two weeks in June passed with quiet marking all activities in the country adjacent to Angel Butte. None appeared to inspect section twenty-two and thus possibly draw the fire of the guards who had been stationed by the combine to protect their dead line. The stranger, camped on the east side of the butte, was seldom seen except by the lookout stationed on the crest of the butte by Martin and the ranchers associated with him.

Amos Brodick now had all his cattle on the summer range within the forest reserve. His men were repairing the irrigation ditches and attending to the distribution of the waters which assured bountiful crops of hay and oats and alfalfa and sedan grass, and nourished a large and varied garden close to the house.

In the vicinity of the little town of Angel, homestead shacks began to appear. The small, unpainted, board structures looked in the sun like splashes of gold against the broad, brown vastness of the prairie country which stretched eastward to the blue rim of the far horizon. Gradually these splashes of gold crept westward toward the rolling flanks of Angel Butte, from the pine-rimmed crest of which the combine's watchers stood vigil.

Neil Sterret apparently was absorbed in the routine activities of the ranch. He spent much time on his horse and made several trips to the Double S, where Lentu treated him with a great show of friendliness and gave him pointers in the use of the weapon which he had obtained from his Uncle Amos, and with which he yearned to become as proficient as the other men of that country. He failed to tell his uncle of these trips or of the glamorous pictures which Lentu painted in Western phraseology of the day when the "good old order of things" would again come into its own.

Dora, visibly pleased with what she considered a good indication of the beginning of Neil's redemption, nevertheless was worried by an intangible feeling of uncertainty and foreboding which appeared to hang in the very air.

Amos Brodick was often preoccupied at meals. She noticed that he never went abroad without his gun, and that the other men of the ranch were constantly armed. The unusual sight of pistol butts banging so close to swinging arms and looking so formidably businesslike carried to her mind a suggestion of impending tragedy—of strife and bloodshed.

She had never mentioned to her uncle the fact that she had witnessed from her window the visit of the mounted men in the night; that the appearance and departure of the unknown man from the east side of the butte was known to her. But she knew these events were much in the mind of her uncle, for since that night he had displayed a stern side to his character and had been much concerned over the slightest of departures from ranch routine; he had held his men under closer rein. His attitude since that night had been one of increasing alertness about the affairs of his domain.

Whether any others on the ranch knew of the night visits she could not be sure, although she suspected that some of the men might be aware of the incident, or Amos Brodick might have told them what he wouldn't think of confiding to his women folks, with whom he ever assumed a cheerful demeanor.

And then one day near the end of June, Neil astonished her by asking his uncle point-blank at the dinner table if he knew the "nester" on the east side of the butte—darting a swift glance of warning at her as he put the question.

"Why do you call this man—whoever he is—a nester?" his uncle countered with a steady questioning gaze.

"That's what people are who—who haven't any business around, isn't it?" demanded Neil, although his face reddened under its fresh tan.

"Nester is a bad word, Neil, my boy," said Amos Brodick kindly. "It's a word that's sort of goin' out of use nowadays. It used to mean a man who came in and squatted on unsurveyed government land; but now there is no cause to call any person by such a name."

"Well, he acts suspicious, doesn't he, Uncle Amos?"

"It isn't anything unusual for a man to come along and camp in this country where there's good fishing and hunting, Neil."

"But it doesn't look right when there's so much work an' everybody's short of hands," Neil protested. "They say this fellow won't work because he doesn't have to work like other folks. They say he's a gunman and a killer and a bandit and too dangerous—"

"Who says that, Neil?" asked Amos Brodick sternly.

Neil's face paled as he saw he had talked himself into a trap. He could not tell his uncle he had heard those sentiments just expressed from Lentu. "Oh— some—of the boys," he replied lamely and covered his confusion by attacking his dinner. "That fire guard who went up on Telltale Peak t'other day said something about it. Guess everybody round here thinks he acts suspicious."

"You must discount anything ill you hear a man in this country saying about another," said Amos Brodick. "Men do not usually say another is a suspicious person without some basis of fact. Mere talk directed at another is liable to be for personal reasons. Just now, with the homestead rush beginning, you're liable to hear most anything—from the combine." He looked at Neil sharply, but the youth did not betray any incriminating interest.

"Has the—the combine got it in for that fellow?" he asked, feigning surprise.

"That I do not know," said Amos Brodick with a frown. "The combine's notions don't interest me, unless—"

Those about the table waited expectantly for him to

complete the sentence, but instead he finished his dinner in silence and went out.

# CHAPTER X
## WARNING THE STRANGER

A LTHOUGH Dora sensed that Neil's statement regarding the stranger on the butte was made partly for her benefit, she could not, for some reason unfathomable to herself, believe that the man with the calm, steady gray eyes and upright bearing, who had championed her cause when Neil had been indiscreet, was in reality a killer—a murderer. Something about him—as she remembered him on the occasion of their chance meeting—seemed to dispute Neil's subtle intimation.

But of these things she had little opportunity to think during the days when preparations were under way for harvesting the crops, when both she and Mrs. French were kept busy in many ways attending to household affairs.

Neil, she felt, was improving. His making over was to be a slow process, but it had unmistakably begun, she reasoned. Thus her days, although constantly overshadowed by vague worries, were not entirely unhappy.

Then came the announcement that the family and most of the hands would go to Angel for the annual Fourth of July barbecue and ball. It had been the custom for years to attend this affair, and the men had asked for the privilege again, Amos Brodick explained. He laughed and joked in a hearty manner in anticipation of the celebration, but Dora saw that under it all he was inclined to be apprehensive.

The men drew straws, and in this way two were selected to remain at home and keep an eye on the ranch and attend to the distribution of the water. It was very warm, and the crops required constant irrigation.

"It'll be some celebration," Neil said to Dora. "An' if that gunman up on the butte takes it into his head to go down to town he's liable to get his head shot off!"

"Neil! Why would any one have cause to do such a thing?"

"I don't like to tell you these things, Dora, but this is a wild country out here, and everybody ain't always what they seem. There's some who think he's a bad man, and that it ain't safe to have him around."

"Have you been talking to some of the men from the other ranches, Neil? I haven't heard any one here say anything about this man, except you."

"You don't see much of the men here, do you?" he countered. "And they wouldn't be telling you things to disturb you. I don't want you to be repeating what I say, but there's liable to be some entertainment that ain't on the program down in Angel on the Fourth."

"Neil, I believe you would like to see something happen!"

"There's got to be things happening in a country like this, and if I don't see some of them I won't know how

68

to act when I get into a mix-up," he explained. "You've got to be ready for anything out here. That's why I wear this gun, and why I'm learning how to use it. It's part of a man's rig out here."

"But, Neil, guns and strange happenings like you— like you hinted might take place in Angel, don't seem to fit in with this peaceful scene around us. The fields and the cattle grazing look a lot like our old home."

"Huh!" he snorted. "You've got more'n one silly notion."

His words kept repeating themselves over and over in her mind and increased her worries that afternoon, so that she decided to ride out into the cool, pine-scented cañon on the eastern side of Angel Butte.

Once more she rode far up the narrow, winding cañon with its pines and firs, its golden slopes whereon grew the berry bushes, ripening now, and with its outcroppings of limestone, resembling carvings high above, or thrusting pinnacles upward until they bore the appearance of spires of celestial cathedrals.

She came upon the stranger suddenly as she turned a bend of the trail about a huge boulder almost covered with vines, with its base in a bed of green kinnikinnick. He was sitting on a ledge of rock idly gazing at the steep slope opposite. His horse grazed near some young alders behind him.

He turned quickly as he heard her horse, and his eyes glowed with surprised recognition, but he spoke no word of greeting.

Dora checked her horse in momentary indecision, while Neil's imputation that it might be dangerous for this man to go to the celebration in Angel flashed through her mind. She was surprised to find herself thinking that she should warn him.

"Nice day," he said finally, removing his hat as she continued to stare.

She started in confusion, and then, speedily making up her mind, she urged her horse toward him.

"There is something which I—I feel I should tell you," she began, conscious of her awkward position. "Something perhaps you should know, although you may think it's—silly." She looked at him doubtfully. He was not one who looked as though he would submit to being shot down without capably resisting.

She was reassured by his laugh, which disclosed a row of white, even teeth; they set off the deep tan of his face to excellent advantage. "What is it you want to tell me?" He smiled up at her as she sat her horse.

But now she found it hard to put into words the warning which she felt it her duty as one human being to another to give him. "Are you—are you planning to—to go down to Angel for the—the celebration?" she faltered.

"Hadn't thought much about it," he confessed.

"You'd better not go!"

"Not go?" He looked much surprised. "An' why not, ma'am?"

"Because you're—you're liable to be—killed."

Again she heard his merry, musical laugh. "I told

70

you you might think it silly," she reproved him a bit haughtily.

Instantly he became serious. "Why do you think I might be killed, ma'am?"

"I cannot tell you why, nor do I know there is any such possibility. I heard something to the effect that there might be trouble in store for you in Angel on the Fourth, and I decided it would be only common decency to—to put you on your guard. Personally I have little interest in the matter."

He rose. There now was no mistaking his seriousness. "I understand, ma'am," he said in a respectful voice, "an' I sure appreciate your kindness. I'll keep my eyes open."

"Then are you going?"

"I just couldn't very well stay away—now." He smiled.

"But it might be very dangerous. I don't know that it would, but—"

"I am not unaccustomed to danger, ma'am," he interrupted. "To get right down to cases I don't mind it a bit. I rather like it!"

"Oh!" The girl's thoughts raced back to Neil's hint that this man was a gunman—a killer. She studied the frank and open features of the man before her. He didn't look bad, she had to confess to herself. She wished she had the courage to question him about himself. "Can you tell me what a gunman is?" she asked suddenly.

The man started. He stared at her searchingly. "I

reckon a man that can get his shootin' iron into action tolerably fast would be a gunman," he replied, continuing to look at her curiously.

"Would he necessarily have had to kill anybody?" she queried timidly.

"Not necessarily, but quite probably," he drawled with a whimsical smile.

For some reason his answer, or the way he said it, seemed sinister—repelling. She could not resist a glance at the worn butt of the pistol which protruded from the holster at his right thigh. Nor was this glance lost upon him. He stepped back a pace, again smiling.

Thoughts of Neil, of his practice with his weapon, came to her. "I wonder if you could tell me: Does the West make bad men?" she asked, spurred on by an earnest impulse for Neil's welfare. "One new to the West," she added quickly, "would it be likely to prove unfortunate for him?"

She thought she caught a gleam of understanding in his eyes as he replied. "Ma'am, the West either makes a man or breaks him thorough. If he has the right stuff in him it makes him every time. Sometimes it makes a bad man over, an' if he can't be made over in the West he can't be made over anywhere, I reckon. The West gets credit, I expect, for a lot of bad men who were bad when they came here—an' got worse. As for the women"—he bowed gracefully and gallantly— "ninety-nine times out of a hundred a woman finds herself out here!"

72

The girl felt her color rising, but again her thoughts reverted to Neil. "But the spirit of the West makes for good, doesn't it?" she asked anxiously.

"The spirit of the West, ma'am, is in her skies, her air, and her land," he said with a sweeping gesture. "You can judge for yourself. It depends on what a person has inside of him."

As he concluded she saw that his face was grim, and that there was a cold, almost harsh look in his eyes.

"Thank you," she said as she wheeled her horse. On the way back down the cañon she felt a thrill as she recalled his last words and the unfathomable air about him as he had said them.

Was this man, then, really dangerous? Was it true that he was a killer? Time and again she pictured with fascinated imagination that worn, black gun leaping into a thin, browned hand and blazing flame and smoke under the shock of crashing bullets. For the first time she thought of him and of the guns with an indubitable feeling of fear. She put spurs to her horse. And as she rode swiftly toward the ranch house she found herself looking forward to the celebration in Angel with undeniable dread.

# CHAPTER XI
## ANGEL MAKES HOLIDAY

EARLY on the morning of the Fourth the ranch was astir with preparation for the journey to town. The day's initial chores were accomplished long before breakfast, which was served fully half an hour earlier than usual both in the men's and the ranch-house dining rooms.

Soon after breakfast several of the men departed, riding horses which had been curried and combed with unusual care and adorned with martingales as a special piece of equipment in keeping with the holiday attire of the men; with their high-crowned hats of plush with colored bands, neckerchiefs of brilliant hues, and shirts of purple and yellow and pink. The holsters, belts, and leather cuffs of the men all were highly polished and ornamented with silver. They made a gay display as they rode away in the golden hour after full dawn.

Dora and Mrs. French, Uncle Brodick's house-keeper, were dressed in holiday garments also, and when Walt Frost drove the buckboard up to the front gate, they donned dusters as a protection against the grime of the road.

Amos Brodick called them and led them to the waiting buckboard, for he had announced that he would himself drive them in. The two women were seated in the second seat, and Amos and Mrs. French's

74

boy, Louis, sat in front.

Neil, resplendent in full Western regalia, with white angora chaps, Stetson, belt, and gun as leading features, came out to see them off, and the balance of the men mounted with Neil and trailed after the buckboard as Amos gave the rein to the horses.

The road up the creek was hard and fine, and they made good time. In less than an hour they were climbing the long acclivity to the west shoulder of the butte. When they reached the summit of the pass, Amos checked the horses and pointed to two buttes far in the northwest.

"Square Butte an' Crown Butte," he said, "and way beyond 'em in the shadow of the big mountains is the Teton country."

Dora thought Mrs. French shuddered as she listened; he looked askance at the elderly housekeeper.

"We used to live there," said Mrs. French.

Amos Brodick turned in his seat to glance at her. "An' well out of it," he said, apparently for her ears alone. "Way in the north you can just see a peak of the Sweetgrass Hills." He pointed with the whip. "Guess they must be most two hundred miles away. An' that streamer of smoke way straight ahead in the prairie is the smoke from the smelter in Great Falls."

Dora breathed deeply at the vast panorama and slowly turned her gaze toward the east, where the town of Angel could be dimly seen. Again she felt a tremor of misgiving. And yet—could this glorious scene of far-flung skies and towering mountains and unending vista of rolling plain, all gold and blue under the bright sun, be merely a setting for tragic deeds, for passions raging unbridled in the minds of men who knew and loved this environment?

Her reverie was interrupted by the resumption of motion. They rode swiftly by the gate of the Double S ranch. No one was in sight. Dora felt better when they had passed and were well on the road which followed the gently undulating slopes down to Angel.

The town was dressed in holiday array after the Western fashion. Scores of small fir and balsam trees had been cut on the timbered slopes of the foothills and were fastened about the fronts of the buildings, tied to posts, and lavished about the interiors of restaurants, saloons, and stores. Bunting hung everywhere with loose ends waving in the gentle breeze, and flags, although in the minority, were given conspicuous places.

A large dancing platform had been erected about two feet from the ground, with a canvas roof, and sides formed by interlacing branches of many fir and balsam trees placed close together and held by scantlings and ropes.

Horsemen rode into town from all directions, and the dust flew in clouds. A band played. Cow-punchers, gay in chaps and bright in colored neckerchiefs and shirts, rode along the main street and thronged the bars. Homesteaders in khaki were in the majority, perhaps, but they gave the men from the ranges a wide berth. Phonographs screeched, glasses tinkled, shouts sounded, spurs jingled, and now and then the general noise was punctuated by the sharp bark of a six-shooter unlimbered in high hilarity.

And over all was the sun and the drifting veils of dust and the blue of clear, high skies, blending with the purple tints of distance, and the vague, indefinable atmospheric exhilaration which is of the West and the West alone. Elbow room and freedom!

Amos Brodick drove to the evergreen-draped entrance of the New West Hotel. "Get a room for the ladies, where they can primp up a bit before dinner," he told the lanky hotel runner who was on duty wearing a large badge that announced the legend, "Commitee."

While Amos went to put up the team, taking the boy, Louis, with him, Dora and Mrs. French were shown to a room which would serve as a headquarters for their stay in town. As the room was at the head of the stairs leading up from the narrow hallway between the bar and the small lobby, they were able to hear with great distinctness the loud talk, laughter, and shouts of the throng below.

Suddenly above the many voices mingled in jest, greeting, and conversation, the two women heard another voice on the stairway which they recognized with a start of interest.

"You don't know what you're saying, Will," said Amos Brodick.

"The devil I don't!" Dora recognized the voice of the man who led the night riders weeks before—the

77

man Amos Brodick had addressed as Martin.

She looked at Mrs. French and saw that the house-keeper also knew the voice and was standing with a hand to her throat and with unmistakable terror in her eyes.

"The devil I don't know what I'm talking about," roared Martin. "You've been my enemy ever since that Sand Creek business, Amos Brodick—tryin' to make out you're better'n I am. You're startin' a feud, Amos, that's what you're doin'—startin' a feud you won't be able to finish."

"Don't talk like that, Martin," pleaded Amos. "I have nothing particular against you—"

"Then why don't you come to the front with McCabe, Pierson, and me? You think you can slip one over on us, an', darn your soul, you can't get over the hill with it!"

"Martin, you're drunk," said Amos Brodick sternly.

"Oh, I'm drunk, am I? I'm drunk because it's the Fourth of July, an' I've got forty men in Angel at my back. I'm drunk because you think you're better'n I am. But I'm a-talkin' cold turkey, Amos, an' you've got to be white or yaller; an' if you're yaller—"

"Now hold on," Amos broke in in a thick voice that quivered with anger. "Don't call me yellow—don't make it more'n I can stand."

"You ain't yaller? You ain't? Then what have you got that gunman staked out up on the butte for? We ain't blind. We can see. What was he down there on twenty-two butting into the play an' takin' sides with the land rats for? What was he doin' up by my place the mornin' after we went down to your ranch to try an' reason with you? Baitin' us—tryin' to start something so he could pull his gun an' do your dirty work—"

"Martin, stop!" cried Amos in a voice trembling with strong emotion. "You don't know what you're saying, an' you'll be sorry for this when you think it over."

"Ain't he your gunman?" demanded Martin thickly. "Ain't he?"

"No—no—*no!*" thundered Amos.

"Well, who is he?" asked Martin.

"I can't tell you who he is—"

"But I can tell you who he is," cried Martin. "He's the Left Hand, that's who he is—which is as much as anybody knows about his name. He's got as many killings behind him as he's got ca'tridges in his belt, an' he's wanted in half a dozen counties, an' you know it. The Left Hand! Wearin' his gun on the right side to pull wool over our eyes. An' you bringin' him over from Meagher County. Thought none of us would spot him. Ratty, the dealer, knew him the second he put eyes on him this mornin', so you—"

"Martin, for the last time, will you stop!"

Mrs. French ran to the door, opened it, and stepped into the narrow upper hall, with Dora close behind her. On the top step stood the boy, Louis.

The housekeeper leaned over the railing. "Amos!" she called.

"Go back," called Amos Brodick.

"Oh, that's all," sneeringly said Martin, who was standing two steps below Amos, halfway down the stairs. "I just wanted you to know, Amos Brodick, that we're on to your play, an' we'll have your gunman before this night's over, an' you'll have to do your dirty work yourself if you're able——"

In one leap, as both Dora and Mrs. French screamed, Amos hurled himself upon Martin. The pair, locked in a seeming death struggle, landed at the bottom of the stairs, and almost simultaneously with the crash of their bodies came the report of a gun.

Dora, white as death, caught the housekeeper as she swooned. Louis ran down the stairs despite her warning to him to come back. Then there was a hurried tramping of many feet, and the cries of men. The girl forced herself to look over the railing.

Amos Brodick, with a crimson stream flowing down his face, was standing back against the wall on one side. Swain, the ranch foreman, was at his side, grim-faced, with eyes narrowed and gleaming. Martin was in the hands of two other men, neither of whom Dora knew. Behind, in the space between the bar and the lobby at the end of the little hallway, many men were jammed. On the floor between Amos Brodick and the man, Martin, was a pistol.

Swiftly Amos reached inside his coat under his left shoulder. He tossed his weapon to the floor beside the one which already lay there.

"Now say the word, Martin, an' we'll go after

them—an' the best man wins!" said Amos in cold, earnest tones.

The men jammed in the hallway backed away. Martin crouched forward, and just as his body became tense for a leap toward the weapons, Lentu pushed his way through the crowd.

One flashing glance at the postures of Brodick and Martin, and he had stepped between them and picked up the guns. He handed Amos his weapon and, keeping Martin's pistol in his own hand, led him quickly away.

Swain and Amos Brodick climbed the stairs. Mrs. French had recovered and was weeping, with her arms about her boy. "Amos," she said as they entered the room, "maybe we better go home."

Without answering her, Amos turned to Swain. "Tell the boys to bunch up and quit drinking. And you better—" He whispered something in Swain's ear in an undertone.

"Do you know where he is?" asked Swain.

"No—find him," replied Amos.

"Don't you think we'd better leave?" Mrs. French asked in a pleading voice.

"Leave? Now? Not if it's my last day on earth!" said Amos Brodick.

# CHAPTER XII
## THE CHALLENGE

AFTER Amos Brodick had cleansed his face, and Mrs. French had cleaned and bandaged the slight wound on his left temple made by Martin's bullet, they went down to dinner.

They ate at one of three long tables piled high with food in the hotel dining room, which was lavishly decorated with evergreens and bunting. Dora noticed that throughout the meal, Swain, the foreman, lingered near the door, and once or twice she saw men from the ranch approach him, speak a few words, and go. She was struck, too, by the fact that Amos had kept them waiting a few minutes until places were available at the lower end of the room, from where he could see all the others in the room.

Mrs. French could not disguise the fact that she was in a veritable torment of worry, and, even after they had left the dining room and were seated with scores of others in a grand stand where they could watch the bucking-broncho contests and other sports, she kept glancing about anxiously and paid scant attention to the feats of Western skill exhibited before them.

After this show came the greased-pig and greased-pole contests, staged in the main street in the open block between the hotel and the depot, and these the party watched from the upper porch of the hotel. There were horse races and roping contests up and down the street, and a parade of all the cow-punchers present, mounted, and riding four abreast.

They saw Lentu in this parade, and Dora heard Amos Brodick mutter: "Paradin' his crowd for my benefit."

"Did you say something, Amos?" Mrs. French asked quickly.

"Nothing," replied the cattleman shortly, although his eyes glinted and he kept looking after Lentu and those riding with him.

When the 3-X-Z men—Brodick's own—passed, with Swain riding at the head, Dora saw Neil with them and clapped her hands. He looked up and waved his hat, his face flushed through the tan, a broad grin on his lips.

Dora was instantly concerned with a peculiarity of his manner—a symptom she had seen before in the Eastern State which they had left. She turned to Amos Brodick.

"Uncle Amos—do you suppose Neil—has—had something to drink?" she faltered.

"Oh, he might have one or two under his belt," Amos said, laughing. "Most of the boys put a few fire-crackers inside of 'em on a day like this to get ready to ride herd on the celebration. But I've shut 'em all off," he added with a frown.

"But Neil promised me he wouldn't drink any more when we came out here," said the girl.

Amos looked at her kindly. "Maybe the boys just naturally talked him into it. They're a hard bunch. Or maybe he's just excited because it's all so new to him. That's probably it."

"I hope so," said Dora, not without a feeling of doubt.

For two hours they watched the various activities in the street while the band played on the porch below them. It was a thrilling, novel sight, this scene of bronzed, active men at play. Nor was Dora the only one who viewed the rodeo with interest. The sides of the street were jammed with homesteaders who watched with amazement as the chapped and spurred wizards of rope and gun and horseflesh cavorted before them.

The soft glow of the sunset was mellowing the skies and sending waves of crimson-tinted color athwart the land when Lentu rode down the street on a beautiful pinto which tripped daintily as if dancing while the band caught the spirit of the exhibition and played, "Put on your old gray bonnet;" and when Lentu made the pinto kneel in the dust of the street so he could lean over its head and brush the ground with his hat the crowd responded with a thundering burst of applause.

This was thought to be the end of the street carnival, but as the throngs began to move they were suddenly arrested by the sight of a tall man arrayed entirely in black from the glistening ebony polish of his riding boots to the crown of his sable hat, riding down the street astride a magnificent black horse.

Horse and rider seemed to blend, except for the

silver trimmings and trappings of the saddle and bridle and the man's modest adornments; and both the animal and its master were the very living embodiment of grace.

The crowd again broke into applause, for in the West a perfect example of spirited horseflesh and a capable, confident master in the saddle are quick to excite admiration and appreciation.

Both Dora and Amos Brodick started in surprise when they recognized the rider.

"Good Lord!" said Amos softly.

But Mrs. French heard him. "Is that the man, Amos?" she asked quickly.

Dora sensed that the housekeeper associated his exclamation with Martin's accusations concerning the stranger on the butte.

Amos Brodick nodded in silence while his gaze roved among the throngs below. Dora leaned close to him, almost breathless with interest and apprehension.

"Will they—kill him?" she heard herself whispering.

"They wouldn't be likely to try it in front of all these people," replied Amos. But Dora noticed that his right hand was inside his coat as he leaned over the porch railing.

The man rode straight down the street until he arrived at the place where Lentu had compelled his pinto to kneel. At this point the rider tossed a silver dollar into the road, to the very spot Lentu had touched with his hat.

He petted the horse gently on the neck while he spoke to him softly and urged him a bit with the spurs. Quickly the animal's four feet came together over the spot where the silver dollar had fallen, and he slowly pivoted—a beautiful sight, and one suggestive of diligent training and perfect understanding between horse and master.

While the band played softly and all eyes admired the feat, Dora found herself instinctively searching for a sight of the big, black pistol butt at his right side. She thrilled with new interest when she saw that it was missing. Then she noticed the rider was holding the rein in his right hand. As the horse swung slowly around, with forelegs crossed, and the left side of the driver was exposed, she suddenly gasped. The gun was there—on *the left side!*

Left Hand! That was what Martin had called him— a gunman with as many killings behind him as he had cartridges in his belt. Could it be possible that this calm, almost boyish-looking man was indeed a ruthless, cold-blooded killer?

Her fascinated gaze lingered on the dull gleams of red which shot from the cartridge-heads in his belt. And instantly she became aware of the fact that this was not a casual exhibition but a challenge from Left Hand to the men who threatened him. The whole performance took on a new and powerful significance.

And now, at a word of command, the horse leaped aside as the rider swung low from the saddle and retrieved the silver dollar from the dust. With the outburst of applause, horse and rider glided up the street and were lost in a cloud of dust shot with the rainbow colors of the sunset.

"Come, folks, we'll go down to supper," said Amos Brodick.

## CHAPTER XIII
### THE ANSWER

WHEN the soft, hazy twilight had deepened into night, and when the great arch of the heavens was spotted with stars, the merrymakers repaired to the dancing pavilion for the climax and end of the celebration, which would last until the first gray banners in the east announced the dawn.

Neil came for Dora to take her to the dance. His face still was flushed, and Dora was soon cognizant of the fact that, whether or not the others from the ranch had ceased their calls at the bars, Neil was patronizing them in defiance of his uncle and with flagrant disregard for his promise to her.

With the knowledge, the old fear came back. Would Neil respond to his new environment, and, more troublesome still, was the environment just what she— they—had expected? The events of the day, coming so swiftly, seemed to presage some far more disquieting happening before the night was over. She observed that several of the men from the ranch appeared to be constantly near Amos Brodick. There was mystery, foreboding in the attitude of her uncle and these men; something sinister in the coincidence of Lentu and Left Hand, as Amos Brodick now unhesitatingly referred to him, taking for a brief moment the center of the stage at the day's celebration. Contemplation of these things temporarily drove from her mind all thoughts of Neil, except such as concerned his safety.

Regardless of what might take place during the night, she would contrive to keep Neil in the dancing pavilion.

Mrs. French accompanied them to the pavilion, stating that Amos Brodick would come along later. Louis was with some young friends. They found the benches along the sides of the place thronged, and dancing was going on as it had been all day.

"I suppose you've heard who your friend is," said Neil when they went upon the floor. "I mean your friend from the butte."

It was the first time he had referred to the incident in the cañon. It had seemed to her in the weeks which followed that he had decided not to mention their unusual situation—to go quietly about the business of redeeming himself and then hold her to her promise, which she felt was fair and creditable in him. Now she chose to disregard his veiled feelings in the matter.

"Neil, I heard the talk that passed between Uncle Amos and that man, Martin," she said quietly; "so I know what they are saying about the stranger."

"Well, he'll get his," said Neil, as they swung into

the dance. "Lentu will attend to him before the night's over!"

"Neil! Do you know what they—Lentu and the others, I mean—plan to do?" she asked quickly.

"Oh, I've heard a few hints dropped," he said significantly.

"Have you told Uncle Amos?"

"Told Uncle Amos?" He appeared surprised. "Why, of course not. It's none of our affair."

"But perhaps he would like to know—what you may have heard. And, if the man is in danger—"

"Why are you so interested in him?" demanded Neil.

"I am not interested in him, Neil, only as—well, I don't hardly believe he is what they say he is, and I don't believe Uncle Amos thinks he is, either. And, anyway, appearances up to now would seem to indicate that he is more on Uncle Amos' side than he is on the other—"

"It isn't a question of sides," Neil interrupted impatiently. "That fellow is known as Left Hand; he's a gunman who's come here to stir up trouble."

"But you don't know that for certain, do you, Neil?"

"Maybe not, but it looks like it; and whatever becomes of him will be all right with me."

Dora was quick to realize that Neil harbored a deep resentment, possibly hatred, against the man for having interfered that day in the cañon. She was dismayed at the thought that she, perhaps, was partly responsible for the animosity shown toward him. She didn't know the facts about his actions against the guards on twenty-two, except as Martin had mentioned them. Was Neil, then, somewhat responsible for the demonstration against the stranger? And the midnight visit after Martin and the others had gone!

"Neil, I am convinced you should tell Uncle Amos all you know."

"I don't know anything," said Neil. "If the fellow was all right why didn't he take a job on one of the ranches? Why is he meddling with the affairs of the combine? Tell me—"

"Why, Neil, the very fact that he is against the combine puts him on the side of Uncle Amos," the girl protested.

"Maybe he's got his reasons," said Neil, almost savagely.

"Neil, don't you see that the combine with Lentu and the others in it are the enemies of Uncle Amos?"

"Maybe they are and maybe not," was his reply. "Uncle Amos might be mistaken. Maybe they're not as bad as he thinks."

Dora stopped the dance and led the way to a vacant place on the bench at the lower end of the floor.

"How can you be so foolish?" she asked him, her eyes flashing. "Neil, have you no inkling as to what is happening about us? Can't you see that the combine is threatening your uncle? Can't you see he is worried and perhaps in danger? Do you know what happened this morning?"

"Swain told me about it," he answered.

"And then you know that Uncle Amos might have been killed by that man, Martin."

"Martin was drunk," said Neil shortly. "If Martin hadn't been drunk nothing would have happened. Anyway, there may be a quarrel between Uncle Amos and Martin that we don't know about. Such things are always happening out here."

"Oh, Neil, I'm afraid you are playing the fool. Such things are not always happening out here. Mrs. French has lived here in this country all her life, and she is worried and apprehensive. There is something beneath it all; maybe it is a quarrel, and we know nothing about it. But whatever it is, Neil, it is serious, and Uncle Amos and perhaps ourselves, are threatened."

"I'll tell you what is behind it," said Neil with an exaggerated gesture and a superior lifting of his brows. "The combine wants Uncle Amos to stick with them against these homesteaders, and this Left Hand has come along and butted into the game."

"But you know why Uncle Amos won't stick with the combine, as you call it, Neil; it is because Uncle Amos does not think they are right. He says they are pushing against a stone wall. We must be loyal to him. We have only been here a short time, and we cannot know exactly what conditions are; we do not yet understand these men and their motives. And if Left Hand is taking part it may be that he is doing so to help Uncle Amos in some way."

"Then why isn't he working on the ranch?" Neil

demanded. "Why doesn't he come out in the open?"

"I cannot answer that, Neil, and neither can you; but I feel that you are incensed against this man because he—he—objected when you—"

"And I've a right to be," said Neil bitterly. "But there's no need to tell everybody this. Here comes Mrs. French."

When the housekeeper joined them Neil excused himself. "I'll be back in a minute," he said. And Dora, at a loss for a reasonable excuse to detain him, watched him go.

Neil entered the nearest saloon, a small place lighted by a single swinging lamp above the bar, which ranged along one side of the short length of the room. Throughout the day he had avoided the Prairie Flower saloon, the first place he had visited after his arrival in Angel. He had not forgotten the incident of the black-jack game when Lentu had come to his rescue in the altercation with Ratty, the ferret-faced dealer. And the dealer's parting fling, "A man's hat don't make a man out of a boob," had burned in his memory. He hated Ratty, for he felt that Ratty had made a fool of him. Even now, as he ordered a drink at the crowded bar, he fingered the butt of the gun in the holster at his right thigh.

This day, attired in cowboy fashion, and mingling with the men from his uncle's ranch and at sly moments with men from the Double S and other ranches of the combine, he had noticed a measure of respectful deference paid him by the men in khaki or overalls from the homesteads. They, like he, were fascinated by the new environment in which they were thrust; but he had the advantage of a make-up—although he discounted this fact if he was aware of it.

While the men from his uncle's ranch tolerated him in friendly fashion, those from the ranches of the combine apparently accepted him as an equal—or treated him as such. They made much of him; invited him to drink with them, listened when he talked, and now and then confided something to him. It was all very flattering. And they told him Left Hand would get his!

As Neil finished his drink he felt a touch on his arm and turned to find Swain behind him. The ranch foreman nodded toward the head of the bar, where there was a little open space between the men drinking at the counter and the front wall of the building near the door. Neil followed Swain to this comparatively quiet location and found two other 3-X-Z men there.

"Bad business to be licking up that stuff, son," said Swain kindly.

Neil resented the fatherly way in which the foreman had always treated him; resented his calling him "son," which seemed to him to be a patronizing term. At times he suspected Swain of humoring him, which was more maddening than all the rest.

"Oh, I guess I can take care of myself," he replied, scowling.

"Against orders today," Swain pointed out. "I suppose your uncle meant to include you with the rest of us."

"Why certainly. I'm one of the outfit, ain't I?" asked Neil, smarting under the imputation that he might not be in the same classification as the others.

"That's why I mentioned it," returned Swain with a smile.

Neil, mollified by this reply, suddenly turned to Swain with an inspiration. "What do you think of this fellow Left Hand?" he asked, striving to veil his intense interest in the subject.

"Don't know much about him," was Swain's cryptic answer.

"Well, what do you think of the grand-stand play he staged this afternoon on the horse up there in the street?"

"Was it a grand-stand play?" countered Swain.

"What else could it be?" sputtered Neil.

"He might have been drawing his enemies out into the open or something like that," Swain intimated, after some hesitation.

"Drawing his enemies out in the open! Rats! He hasn't come out in the open himself, has he?"

"That's according to how you look at it," replied Swain, although he did not offer to explain what he meant by his answer.

"They'll probably send Lentu after him," observed Neil, watching the foreman closely to ascertain the effect of this. But Swain remained silent.

"Has anybody seen Left Hand since his stunt in the street?" Neil asked.

"I suppose so," Swain answered evasively.

"Maybe he's lit out of town to avoid trouble."

"Think so?"

"I heard—happened to overhear—a couple of combine men saying that Lentu would drift into every saloon in town tonight looking for him," Neil asked.

"Well, he may have a chance to see him right here," was Swain's astonishing reply.

"Is—is Left Hand coming in here?" gasped Neil.

"No, he ain't coming—he's here," said Swain, pointing cautiously toward the distant end of the bar.

Neil looked in the direction indicated and saw the man called Left Hand standing close to the end of the bar. He had his particular nook pretty much to himself, and he was standing with his back to the bar. Neil saw there was an open door in the rear of the place, apparently leading into a back yard. Left Hand kept his gaze darting at frequent intervals from the back door to the front of the room, yet his attitude was that of one merely lounging in lazy fashion after a drink or two.

Although Neil thoroughly hated this man for his interference between him and Dora in the cañon on the east side of the butte, he nevertheless respected the reputation that the combine's men had given him. He was thrilled by sight of the weapon strapped securely to the man's left thigh; thrilled more at the prospect of a meeting between this man and Lentu, another reputed gunman of lightning ability and accuracy. Would there be trouble? Neil fervently hoped so.

As if in answer to his unvoiced wish there was a

commotion in the front doorway. Martin, of the Double S, entered, with an authoritative-looking man at his side, and followed by several of the combine's employees.

"There he is," shouted Martin, pointing out the man at the lower end of the bar. "Know him?"

The crowd broke away from the bar, leaving an open space in which Martin and the men with him confronted the stranger.

"Can't say that I know him," said the authoritative-looking man coldly.

"No?" roared Martin. "Well, that's Left Hand, wanted in half a dozen counties. Now, Mr. Deputy Sheriff, what you going to do about it?"

The officer stepped forward a pace. Instantly the smiling face of the man with his back to the bar froze in grim lines, and his eyes narrowed.

"What's your name?" demanded the deputy.

"Smith!" The word seemed to crackle, it came so short.

"Smith!" echoed Martin in a jeering voice. "Do you see where he wears that gun, sheriff—on his left side? Do you—"

"There's more'n one left-handed man in these parts, Martin," interrupted the deputy. It was plain he was not unmindful of the menace which shone from the eyes of the man accused. "And I'm not goin' to accept an identification if it's no better'n on the word of Ratty, that crooked little dealer."

"That's up to you," retorted Martin as the deputy

swung on his heel and departed. "Scared stiff," he added savagely.

"How about yourself?" Left Hand asked with an amused smile.

"I'm an old man," Martin began, but ceased speaking as another pushed in front of him.

Neil held his breath as a hushed silence fell over the whole room. The faint strains of music from the dancing pavilion and occasional noises from the street outside were all that disturbed the stillness as Lentu confronted his man.

It was the first time these two men had met face to face. Lentu was scowling ominously, his chin out-thrust, while the other appeared to smile grimly, yet with something hinting of keen satisfaction, though his eyes glowed with a sinister light.

Lentu leaned a bit forward, his scowl wearing away as he stared intently at the other. "Left Hand?" he murmured, half to himself, yet loud enough for all in the house to hear.

"The same," was the unexpected, startling answer, given with another smile, in cool, clear tones.

The two men remained motionless, standing in a half crouch, arms and hands tensed for lightning strokes at the slightest indication of action on the part of one or the other.

Men who were minded to move away remained rooted to the spot in fascination. Five seconds, that seemed an eternity, slipped by, and suddenly from the front of the room came three shots. The room was plunged into darkness as the glass from the shattered swinging lamp fell to the floor. And with the sound of the falling glass came darting streaks of fire and the sharp thunder of exploding cartridges; then followed stillness and the pungent odor of pistol smoke and a slow, gasping sound as men recovered their breath.

"Strike a light!" It was Lentu's voice.

There was a shuffle of feet behind the bar, and an extra lamp was lit.

Its pale gleam disclosed Lentu standing in the open space with a gun in his right hand. Left Hand was nowhere to be seen. Lentu shoved the weapon into its sheath and pushed his way out of the crowd.

Neil surged through the front doorway with the throng which was leaving. In the open air he stood looking about him with a vague stare, thoroughly sobered by what he had seen, and with the new and amazing burden of knowledge which was his.

What did it mean? Why—why—why? He kept asking himself this as he slowly made his way toward the dancing pavilion. Gradually, as his senses became normal, he remembered; and with remembrances he felt the sharp prod of a painful curiosity.

The three shots which had shattered the lamp had come from almost over his right shoulder. He had stepped forward half a pace when Lentu had entered. And Swain had been standing at his right side!

# CHAPTER XIV
## THE SAND CREEK HANGING

SHORTLY after midnight Mrs. French, Amos Brodick's housekeeper, prevailed upon Dora to return to their room in the hotel to get some rest. She explained that such affairs as the celebration dance always increased in good-natured violence toward morning—a violence to which Dora was unaccustomed and by nature antagonistic—and that Amos would be around to call them for breakfast before daylight in order to get an early start for the ranch.

She might have spared herself the long explanation, for Dora was quite ready to retire to their room. The excitement of the day had so troubled her thoughts that her brain seemed numbed to further mental effort. She had heard about the meeting between Lentu and Left Hand, and Amos Brodick had advanced the confidential information that Left Hand was unhurt and had left town. She refused to concern herself any further about the matter.

Neil had appeared thoughtful and absent-minded—something she attributed to the after-effect of what he had consumed in some under-cover, law-defying place, and the thought caused her disgust. He told her Swain had said that Martin and most of his men had ridden away. He had seemed repentant of his former aggressive belittling of her theories and arguments, but this had given her no satisfaction, and she said good night to him with relief.

When the women reached their room they found Mrs. French's boy, Louis, already asleep in a cot at the foot of their bed. Dora undressed wearily, but after they had gone to bed she tossed and turned in restless contemplation of the many disturbing angles to the series of events which had transpired since she and Neil had arrived at the Brodick ranch.

"You must try to get some sleep, deary," said Mrs. French. "Close your eyes and forget everything."

But the woman's tone told Dora that she, too, was worried and thinking. She felt a bond of sympathy between herself and the elderly housekeeper who had always been so kind to her.

"I can't sleep, Mrs. French; I just can't. If I knew what it was all about I would feel easier. And, Mrs. French, what could that man Martin have meant this morning when he said Uncle Amos had been his enemy ever since that Sand Creek business, and that Uncle Amos thought he was better than Martin was himself?"

"Hush, deary; you must never mention that 'less you whisper."

"But what is it, Mrs. French?" Dora persisted. "Can't you tell me? You can trust me if it shouldn't be repeated."

"Oh, there's plenty who know about it," said the housekeeper. "But it isn't talked about very much. There'd be no harm in telling you, but I'm afraid it would upset you, dear."

"Mrs. French, I would like to hear about it. If it is in some way responsible for the actions of those men toward Uncle Amos I would like to know about it. I am sure I wouldn't worry so much if I knew everything; and if I can't know everything, I do want to know as much as I can. Of course I cannot insist that you tell me unless you feel free to do so."

Dora sensed that Mrs. French was really aching to unburden herself of the story and was content to wait until she should begin. Presently the woman rose to make sure that the boy, Louis, was asleep.

"Do you remember yesterday morning"—it was now long after midnight—"when we reached the top of the pass over Angel Butte, dear?" asked Mrs. French.

"When Uncle Amos was pointing out the landmarks in the distance? Yes, I remember; and didn't you say you used to live somewhere up north—"

"In the Teton country," supplied Mrs. French. "Your uncle, you'll remember, said we were well out of it. He was right. I always shudder when I think of what happened up there. Yet it was the finest country I was ever in—or it seemed that way to me; long stretches of nearly level range with the mountains close behind. My Louis was born up there. His father worked for your uncle. After he was kicked so badly by a wild horse and died from it I became your uncle's housekeeper, and he has always been good and kind to Louis and me. Amos Brodick is a fine example of a real Western gentleman, dear.

"One night when we were living up there some men came to the ranch and asked for your uncle. They talked to him in the little front room off the parlor that he used for an office. It seemed that two men had stolen some mules—at least the men who came to see Amos claimed the mules had been stolen. They said the suspects claimed to have brought the mules down from Canada, but that it was a lie, for the men had abandoned them and started north when they found they were exciting suspicion.

"Your uncle went with the men to a conference at a near-by ranch where it was decided to follow the two men accused of stealing the mules. I have heard two sides to the story which was told by the suspects. One was that they had brought the mules down from Canada, as I told you; and the other was that they had taken the mules from a man who owed them a big sum in wages which he refused to pay. I don't know which is the true story—if either of them is true.

"But Amos thought there was something else behind the business. He said it looked to him as though some of the men were enemies of the two accused of stealing the mules. Anyway, he proposed that they notify the proper authorities and send them after the two men and bring them to trial. His suggestion was sneered down, and when he saw the bitterness shown he refused to join in the chase and came back to the ranch. Two of the men rode part way back to the ranch with him, entreating him to join them, and even threatening him, but he would have nothing to do with the matter.

"Well, the others went after the two suspects. They finally cornered them in a cabin near Sand Creek, which used to be in the reservation. The men in the cabin stood the posse off with their guns, and finally one of the posse advanced to talk with them under a flag of truce, which was a white handkerchief or something tied to a stick.

"This man told the pair in the cabin that they were cornered and outnumbered and didn't have a chance to get away. But he said the posse had decided to give them a chance to defend themselves in the courts, and that if they would give themselves up the members of the posse would see that they were safely transported to Fort Benton, where they would be given a fair trial on the charge of having stolen the mules, and would be released if they were innocent.

"The men said a fair trial was what they wanted and denied they had stolen the mules and said they had fled because of the hostile way the posse had acted. So the man with the flag of truce repeated the promise that they would be taken safely to Fort Benton to be given a fair trial and released if found not guilty. Then the two suspects, assuming that the word of the posse was good, just as the word of most men in the West is good, gave themselves up."

Again Mrs. French rose and bent over the cot where Louis was lying, to make sure he was asleep.

"When the men surrendered, the members of the

posse were surprised to find that they had a boy with them," the housekeeper continued in a very low voice. "They didn't know the name of the boy or the names of the men, either. They took the weapons which the two suspects had and put a guard in front of the cabin in which were the suspects and the boy. He was only a young boy—about nine or ten years old. Just about Louis' age.

"That night the other members of the posse made the guard stand with his face to the cabin wall, and then they went up behind him and blindfolded him. They told the men in the cabin to come out and quickly tied their hands behind their backs. Then they took them to a cottonwood tree and, without giving them a chance, hanged them!"

Dora cried out in horror. "Hanged them after they had promised— Oh, Mrs. French, that was terrible!"

"Hanged them until they were dead, after they had got them to surrender with a flag-of-truce promise to see that they got a fair trial," said the housekeeper. "And they drove the little boy out upon the prairie in the dead of night—alone and without food. He was never seen or heard of again! In after months bones were found in the vicinity, which showed that the boy had died on the prairie or had been killed by wolves and his flesh eaten by the wild animals."

"Oh, that was horrible, Mrs. French. What did they do to the men who were in the posse?"

"The law was not very strict," replied the house-keeper. "It was hushed up. I think they did have some kind of hearing about it, but there was not enough evidence. The story leaked out bit by bit, but it could never be proved just who were responsible."

"But Uncle Amos knew who they were, didn't he?"

"He knew some of them—yes," whispered Mrs. French. "But even if he had decided to testify he would never have lived to reach the witness stand. The affair turned public sentiment against the unknown members of the posse, and they would have killed your uncle rather than let him live to testify against them. And not only would your uncle's life have been at stake if he had been minded to tell what he knew, but his cattle would have been run off or killed, and he had to protect his bankers, to whom he owed a large sum at that time. Pressure was brought to bear on him through these bankers, for the members of the posse had influence behind them, and many were said to be prominent."

"And how does that business affect Martin and uncle's relations?" asked Dora, although she suspected the truth.

"Don't ever tell a soul that I told you this," cautioned Mrs. French in a faint whisper. "Martin was one of the posse, and his man, Lentu, who was young then, was the leader!"

"Oh," said Dora softly, "I begin to see."

"Two years after the hanging we moved away from up there, and your uncle bought the place south of Angel Butte. Later, when the homesteaders began to appear in the country north, and there was talk of irrigation, Martin and McCabe moved down this way, too. Martin and Lentu know your uncle knows much about the affair they were mixed up in, and although it happened many years ago, and is very seldom talked about now, Martin has always thought your uncle would tell what he knew before he died. Your uncle hasn't had much use for Martin or Lentu since that business up north."

"Were any of the others of the combine in that affair?" Dora asked.

"I don't know, deary, although I suspect McCabe. I wouldn't be surprised if they were, though. And I've believed lately that they want to get Amos involved in this homestead war so that he will be equally guilty with them if anything should happen, and so seal his lips about the other. But I think your uncle believes in letting bygones be bygones, as he told Martin, and has never thought of telling what he knows."

"Mrs. French, do you believe Uncle Amos has hired this gunman, Left Hand, to protect him, or for any other purpose?"

"No," replied the housekeeper quickly. "I know Amos Brodick, and I know he wouldn't hire any one else to fight his battles. Now, deary, we must try to get some sleep, for we'll have to start for the ranch in three or four hours. Do try to sleep."

But Dora found herself at dawn still pondering the riddle of the man in black with the gun strapped to his left thigh.

# CHAPTER XV
## THE COMBINE PREPARES

WHEN Swain told Neil that Martin and most of his men had ridden out of town he was mistaken. Several of the Double S and other combine men did ride away, but Martin and Lentu met within an hour after the affair with Left Hand in a small room over the Prairie Flower saloon.

"A fine mess you made of things," Martin accused when they had lighted the little lamp in the place and stood facing each other.

"Now don't start that line of talk," said Lentu savagely.

"Why, not? You didn't go through!"

"That lamp being busted was enough to throw anybody off his guard," growled Lentu, settling his big frame in a chair, and staring at the lamp on the small table with its greasy oilcloth cover.

"Sure it was; but it gave you a chance to get him. You shot six times—I counted the shots; and you missed him every time!"

"Because it was dark an' he ducked," Lentu said, snarling.

"Of course he ducked. Got plumb away in clean fashion. But you didn't duck, Lentu. He could have potted you by the flashes of your gun as easy as not— easier, maybe."

"But he didn't," observed Lentu, not without a show

of genuine surprise at the fact of his life being spared at the very moment he was trying to kill another—and by his intended victim.

"He could have dropped you where you stood," said Martin.

"That's twice you've said that," said Lentu angrily.

"Well, what do you make of it?" Martin inquired, sitting down in a chair across the table from his right-hand man.

"Brodick's scheme. Probably decided it would look too raw—if Left Hand could have got away with it."

Martin laughed sneeringly. "He couldn't have helped getting away with it if he'd wanted to plug you. And all my work bringing that deputy around so he could see this Left Hand was a gunman and give you some excuse for putting him out—forced to draw— for nothing. Lentu, it looked to me as if you was sort of rattled and maybe—maybe—"

"Don't say it," warned Lentu with a dangerous gleam in his eyes.

"Well, I won't," decided Martin. "Only— Well, I've never seen you hesitate before, and—"

"Maybe I saw more'n you did," growled Lentu, again becoming thoughtful. "But we'll let that go. I wonder who shot the light out."

"Why, I thought one of the boys shot it out when he saw the play was hanging fire, to give you a better chance," said Martin. "One of our boys, I mean."

"Like fun one of our boys did!" shouted Lentu. "Martin, you're gettin' raw. None of our boys shot that light out. I took pains afterward to ask 'em. They was all right behind me and you, an' the shots came from behind them."

Martin frankly was puzzled. He stared at Lentu in astonishment. "Well, who could have shot it out, then?" he asked in bewilderment.

"Some of Brodick's crowd, likely," replied Lentu.

"But what good did it do 'em? Left Hand didn't try to take advantage of it, unless it was to get away."

"That's just it," said Lentu earnestly. "He took advantage of it to duck an' get away. Didn't want to shoot it out with me, probably." But Lentu's last words did not carry any great conviction, and Martin noticed this.

"That feller's got a reputation of bein' able to shoot just as fast as he can think," said Martin dryly.

"Then why didn't he start to draw in the first place?" Lentu insisted. "I was ready for him. I expected it. I was just going for my own gun when the light popped out."

"If that light was shot out by one of Brodick's men it was because they didn't want a killin' between you two fellers just now," said Martin in a convincing tone. "Whichever of you fellers is the fastest with your shootin' iron, an' I strongly hope you are, they didn't want any fatality at present. Now that's the upshot of the whole business—if one of Brodick's men shot the light out."

But Lentu was hardly listening to him. He was musing. "I believe—there—was—another reason," he said slowly and softly. "But I'm not going to be fool enough to tell anybody—no, not even you. Say, Martin, this game is going faster and further than we thought—ain't it?"

"You just finding that out?" Martin asked, sneering. "You're not gettin' cold feet, are you?"

"Stop that kind of talk, Martin," said Lentu sharply. "None of us can get cold feet now. If anybody shows any signs of laying down, I'll—"

He ceased talking and rose to his feet as a peculiar knock sounded on the door. Then he opened the door to admit McCabe.

"He's cleared out," said McCabe as soon as the door was closed. "Lit out on that black horse of his goin' north, an' none of the men could keep him in sight. That's some piece of horseflesh. Wonder where he had him cached?"

"Oh, that's nothing," said Martin. "That's just one of the things to wonder about that feller. Looks to me like he's got us all buffaloed," he added with a grin at Lentu.

"Yes? Maybe he has." McCabe spoke angrily. "Well, you sure made a smart play this mornin', Martin; goin' after Brodick that a way an' talkin' your fool head off."

"Never mind that," said Lentu sharply. "I've explained all that to him. He says he's willin' to take a little valuable advice from now on."

"Good thing," observed McCabe. "Maybe we all need some of that. Learn anything more about who shot the light out, Lentu?"

Lentu shook his head. "But I ain't quit tryin' to find out," he remarked. "Things have got to move sprightly from here on. Listen—"

For half an hour the three men spoke in whispers, seated about the table with their heads close together. Finally Lentu rose to his feet, started toward the door, and then suddenly swung to confront the others. "An' if any of the bunch starts to feeling bashful about the game," he began, "he'll—"

He nodded silently and went out.

An hour or more after midnight, Neil, feeling the reaction from the excitement and indulgences of the day, slipped quietly out of the dancing pavilion and made his way to the little barroom where had occurred the meeting between Lentu and Left Hand.

The place held a peculiar fascination for him. The sight of the two men facing each other, of their tenseness and the breathless air of expectancy, the sudden shots from over his shoulder, the darkness and the sharp cracks of Lentu's gun—all burned in his memory.

He knew, deep down in his heart, that he had wanted to see gun play; that he would have given speed to Lentu's draw if he could have done so by thinking. He hated Left Hand. He had begun to believe that the man was a hero in Dora's eyes.

There were not many in the place, and none of the 3-X-Z men—Brodick's outfit—was there. Neil gave his order, and he had not consumed it before he was joined by Lentu.

"Believe I'll have one myself, old-timer, if you don't mind drinking with me," said the Double S foreman genially.

Neil felt flattered, for all eyes were upon his companion. When Lentu looked slowly about, however, the others in the place turned again about their business.

"Tough luck you ran up against tonight," Neil volunteered.

"That was a bit tough," agreed Lentu after they had finished. "Have another, Sterret; I'm feeling sort of reckless myself, an' you seem to be the only one in Brodick's crowd who ain't afraid to celebrate like a man."

Inwardly and outwardly Neil glowed. A man's praise, this was!

"There's only one thing botherin' me," said Lentu in an undertone as they again had recourse to the refreshment the bartender surreptitiously slid toward them. "I can't figure out who fired the shots that smashed the lamp."

"Spoiled your chance to get your man, didn't it?" Neil suggested as they drank.

"It sure did—an' it would have been good riddance to have dropped that hombre," said Lentu.

Neil's hatred against Left Hand again flared red.

"The shots came from around me somewhere," he said softly.

"Yes, guess they did," drawled Lentu without looking at Neil. "Must have been some friend of his back there."

"Would you go after the man who smashed the lamp if you knew who he was?" asked Neil with real concern.

"Oh, I wouldn't say that," said Lentu. "Only I'd know what to look out for the next time. Can't say I care so much who used the lamp for a target; just curious to know if it was one of our gang."

"I don't believe it was," said Neil craftily, pouring himself another drink. The next time! Did Dora think Left Hand was a hero? Was she glad for more than one reason that the man had interfered between them?

"No, I don't hardly think either that it was one of our crowd," Lentu was saying. "Still, you never can tell."

"I'm quite sure it wasn't," said Neil. The next time! He looked at Lentu with fresh interest. This man had been his friend, hadn't he? The other had been—

"Lentu, those shots came from over my shoulder," said Neil in a low voice, vibrant with suppressed excitement.

"That so?" said Lentu, affecting but a mild interest.

"Yes. They came from over my right shoulder. I was standing beside a man just before you came in and when you came I stepped a bit ahead of him."

"Oh, that doesn't mean whoever you was standing near fired 'em," said Lentu. His tone might have indicated to Neil that he was but little concerned; but the youth could not see the glitter in his eyes, for they were centered upon the glass he held in steady fingers. "I don't suppose you remember who that man was, anyway."

"Yes, I do. It was Swain," said Neil quickly.

"Oh, well, it doesn't make much difference," drawled Lentu.

Two minutes afterward they parted, Neil going back to the dancing pavilion, and Lentu crossing the street.

Lentu went directly to the Prairie Flower. He found Martin and McCabe at the bar. "Swain fired the shots at the lamp," he told them crisply. "I got the truth out of young Sterret."

A short interval of silence greeted this announcement.

"That don't leave any doubts as to who Left Hand's working for," said McCabe.

"And don't leave us any too much time," put in Lentu. "I'll get the bunch together, an' we'll slope."

In the hour before dawn the stillness of the west end of the main street was broken by the pound of hoofs. Dora, lying sleepless, rose upon her pillow and looked out of the window. She saw a number of riders racing in the moonlight; watched them until they merged with the shadows which slanted across the first easy slopes at the foot of Angel Butte.

# CHAPTER XVI
## THE FIRST STROKE

IT was Walt Frost who drove Dora, Mrs. French, and the boy, Louis, to the ranch early in the morning. Amos Brodick saw them off and explained that he could not go back to the ranch that day, as he had some business to attend to in The Falls, which would necessitate his going to the smelter city. He said he would return the next day and instructed Walt to leave his horse in Angel for him to use when he came back.

Swain, Neil, and the others of the men started for the ranch at daybreak and reached home before nine o'clock. After a second breakfast in the bunk-house dining room, Swain announced that he would ride up Wild Horse Valley to look after the upper herd which was grazing near the head of the creek and would likely have to be moved in a few days to fresh range.

Neil had the length of the irrigation ditch up the valley—some six miles—to ride, as the daily inspection of the ditch was one of his regular duties. Swain, riding fast so that he could complete his inspection and return to the ranch that night, left him at the end of the upper pastures and pushed on. Neil rode leisurely along, keeping a casual eye upon the amount of water in the ditch, and pausing momentarily at the flumes which occasionally wound around some point of rock or bridged a low place. He found everything in good order and the leakage remarkably small, considering the hot, dry weather which had been the rule during June, instead of the rainfall which he had been told was usual during that month each year.

As he made his way up the creek on the fine, hard trail, with the greens of pine and fir on the slopes of the mountains which hemmed in the little valley, shining in welcome contrast to the sear browns and yellows of the grass and gravel in the open spaces near the creek, he noted the general dryness of the forests and remembered the warning of the fire guard who had been sent up to Telltale Peak to be careful about matches and burning cigarettes.

He dismounted frequently for long, cooling drafts of the clear water in the creek—the nectar of mountain springs. He liked to mount and dismount, to hitch up his chaps and gun belt, to take off his wide-brimmed, high-crowned hat for a glance of satisfied admiration while he mopped his brow with the huge bandanna he carried in a hip pocket.

Neil liked to ride, too, for he was becoming adept in the saddle, and, in addition to its being a novelty to him, it gave him a chance to give free rein to his imagination. Today, with the memory of the events of the day before fresh in his mind, he could see himself as the aggressor against such men as Left Hand and Ratty, perhaps—a pair whom he hated thoroughly.

Eventually he came to the end of the irrigation ditch, where the water was taken from Wild Horse Creek.

Everything was all right, and here he dismounted, threw the reins over his horse's head so the animal could drink and graze, loosened the saddle cinch, and then, taking the bit of lunch he had brought along tied on the cantle of the saddle with the ever-present and most-times superfluous slicker, he sat down in a little clump of aspens and firs for a bite and an hour of lazy leisure.

As he ate and then leaned against a tree, Neil considered the problem of his situation with his wife Dora. If she was infatuated with Left Hand, as he had begun in a narrow, jealous way to suspect, it was probable that such an obstacle between them would be removed sooner or later by Lentu; for Lentu had sworn to get the newcomer and had impressed Neil with his vaunted ability to do so. Indeed Neil was prepared to assist him, if opportunity should offer.

He had purposely refrained from thrusting his attention upon Dora, believing that in time she would "come round" to his way of thinking. It was a silly business and would have to end some time. She would be sensible enough to see that before the year was up. And doubtless as he grew more familiar with the ways of the West, and became more like the men of the country, she would come to look upon him differently—with more respect.

It would all adjust itself in time, he reasoned. And when the time was ripe he would convince her that her attitude in the matter was foolish and futile and unfair, and she would give in. That would end it. He wanted

Dora, of course; he had no semblance of doubt in his mind on that score.

As the afternoon wore on, Neil prepared to go back down the creek to the ranch. However, it was always with regret that he left the upper parts of the valley, for he loved the sight of the pine-clothed mountains crowding in and the silence and open vistas between the trees up the creek. In this instance he remembered that his uncle was not at the ranch, and it would not matter in any event if he was a little late in returning. Two miles above was a point where the walls of the valley narrowed, nearly cutting it in halves, save for a gap between the cliffs.

Why shouldn't he go on up the creek into the upper half of the valley and meet Swain and ride back to the ranch with him?

He debated the matter for a minute and decided that was what he would do. It was a glorious day, cool in the upper reaches of the valley, and the ride back to the ranch in the twilight would be delightful.

So he tightened his saddle cinch, mounted, and turned his horse up the trail which led through the gap toward the head of the creek. Neil had been to the head of the creek once before and knew approximately where the upper herd of cattle was grazing. He half expected to meet Swain coming back, but about two hours afterward he found himself at the place where the trail to the bench on which the cattle were grazing led off from the creek, and he had not seen anything of Swain.

He turned to his right and followed the broad trail to the top of the ridge on that side where a broad bench-land reached northward for several miles—a plateau covered with excellent grass. The beef cattle were supposed to be using this range. But Neil sat his horse and stared in amazement across the tableland. He looked east and west and north—scanned every foot of ground with his startled gaze and muttered to himself in astonishment.

There was not a single head of cattle in sight! The plateau was bare of stock, without a living thing to greet the eye on any portion of it.

"Where—have—they—gone?" Neil said aloud to himself.

Had Swain decided this range was so well eaten off that it was no longer suitable for the upper herd? The range didn't look so bad, Neil reflected. And had Swain moved, or attempted to move, the cattle alone? Impossible! The upper herd included more than three hundred head. Neil turned his horse and looked across the little valley to summits of the mountains opposite. He started in surprise as he looked, and his gaze froze.

Almost directly across from where he sat his horse was the pass which led over the divide toward the Smith River country. And on the slope of a mountain behind the lap of the pass he saw numbers of slowly moving objects—cattle!

And, as he watched the movement of the cattle in puzzled surprise, he saw a number of white puffs of smoke appear and drift in veils until they were dissolved by the breeze. He heard several dull, reverberating echoes. The movement of the cattle apparently increased in speed. Pistol shots and running cattle!

Instantly there flashed across Neil's thoughts a word with which he had conjured—rustlers!

His uncle's cattle had disappeared; there were now cattle in the mountains south of Wild Horse Creek where there had been none before; those cattle were moving toward Smith River, and pistol shots were urging them on.

He drove his spurs into his horse and plunged down the trail to the creek. And now he noticed something which had escaped his attention on the way up. The tracks on the trail had the appearance of having been freshly made—within a few hours—that day! He had seen no cattle on the way up the creek, although he had heard his uncle declare that the beef herd when it moved would move down the creek into the pastures before shipping. No, there was little doubt in Neil's mind but that the band of stock south of Wild Horse was Amos Brodick's beef herd. And, as he reached the narrow floor of the valley, splashed through the creek, and speedily began the long climb on the other side, a new and more wildly startling theory formed in his excited mind.

Might it not be that Swain himself, taking advantage of Amos Brodick's absence from the ranch, was trying to make away with the cattle?

So excited was Neil that he did not notice the dying sun in the western skies as he urged his horse up the trail. And when he reached the pass he was more or less astonished to find that the twilight was beginning to fall—the long, hazy twilight of the high hills, when the colors of the sunset lay upon the trees and ground with the thickness of a shroud or a carpet.

He galloped through the pass and came in sight of the herd. It was milling on the lower slope of a mountain above the wide trail which led down the southwest side of the divide. Neil's view of the trail below was shut off by an outcropping of limestone on the left and a thick growth of timber on the right.

As he checked his horse in sudden indecision the sharp staccato of a volley of shots sounded below and ahead of him. He rode to the farther side of the limestone, where he could see the trail for a short distance. Here he halted again, uncertain as to how to proceed in a situation with which he was unfamiliar, and under circumstances in which he had had no experience.

Just as he had made up his mind to ride slowly ahead until he could see what was going on, he heard another volley of shots. A moment afterward a rider came into view, thundering up the trail, twisted in his saddle and firing at some invisible target behind him. Almost with the echoes from his shots the rider dropped his weapon, sagged in his saddle, toppled to one side, and fell in a crumpled heap upon the dust of the trail almost at Neil's horse's feet as his mount thundered madly on, riderless and thoroughly frightened.

Struck motionless and dumb with his first sight of

tragedy, Neil stared down at the white features and wide-open, unseeing eyes of the man lying twisted in the trail. Terror was mirrored in his fixed gaze as he recognized the dead man.

It was Swain, the foreman.

Before Neil could fully comprehend the significance of this knowledge he again heard the rapid pound of hoofs and raised his head in time to see three other riders come into view—the leader with a gun in his right hand held up level with his head and tipped back over his right shoulder.

Quickly the gun snapped forward, but in the very act of firing, the man tipped its muzzle so that the bullet went wild. His eyes started with surprise as he brought his horse to a rearing halt, and from his throat issued a gurgle of inarticulate oaths.

The two men behind him drew up close to their leader, who continued to stare first at the body of Swain upon the ground and then at Neil, looking at him in horrified fascination.

"You happened along just in time," said the leader, sheathing his gun. "Right on the spot."

"Lentu!" cried Neil, for the leader was indeed the Double S foreman. "Lentu—you've killed Swain!"

# CHAPTER XVII
## SHADOWS OF DOUBT

L ENTU and Neil stood by their horses at the head of the valley wherein flowed Wild Horse Creek. The soft mantle of night had fallen over the mountains, but its canopy, which arched above the serrated outlines of the towering ridges, was aglow with stars, and the floor of the valley was bathed in a pale light.

Lentu had taken his cue from Neil's question as to what Swain, the foreman, had been up to.

"Of course he was tryin' to steal the herd," Lentu was saying. "We was crossin' the divide to see about some cattle that's for sale over on Smith River an' caught Swain driving the bunch through the pass. When we asked him where he was takin' 'em he started shootin'. Then we knew something was wrong an' took after him. You saw what happened. We didn't intend to drop him; we was only tryin' to stop him."

Neil shook his head in perplexity. The sight of violent death up there in the hills—the death of a man whom he had known intimately—shocked him and left him nearly speechless.

"Now look here, Sterret," Lentu continued, "you know this fellow Left Hand ducked out of Angel mighty quick last night, ridin' north. He an' Swain probably had it made up to get away with Brodick's cattle. Like as not he cut around over the hills an' made it to the other side of the divide an' is coming back up the trail to meet Swain, he thinks, an' help him. That's probably why Swain was so anxious to see him get away down in Angel that he shot the lamp to pieces to stop me killin' him. It looks mighty like a frame-up, doesn't it? Of course it does! Now I'll take my two men an' drill on down the trail on the other side, an' maybe we'll hit up with this Left Hand. If we do we'll fetch him in, some way. If we don't we'll lay for him an' some time find out what he had to do with this business."

"But, what'll I do?" asked Neil in apprehension.

"Go right back to the ranch," said Lentu. "Tell 'em you saw the cattle bein' moved in the pass an' took up there an' saw Swain chasin' 'em an' firin' his gun, an' then he came ridin' up to you firin' an' fell off his horse beside you dead."

"And what'll I say to them about you and—"

"Don't say anything about us," said Lentu harshly. "Just forget you saw us at all. That's the only way we can corner the other man. You better tell 'em when you get to the pass you found Swain layin' there dead."

"But maybe they'll think I—that I—I killed him," Neil stuttered. "It looks bad for me!"

"Not unless you go tryin' to blame it on somebody else," replied Lentu quickly. "If you was to tell 'em you saw us, for instance, we'd just prove an alibi— which we can do, for nobody saw us come up here— an' that would make it look bad for you. But they'll know you didn't do it; don't worry. An' even if some

124

fool person was to think you did it he couldn't prove anything. You're safe so long as you stick to the story I told you—comin' up here an' seein' Swain chasin' the cattle an' then findin' him dead."

"They may think it's funny I didn't try to bring the body back to the ranch," said Neil doubtfully.

"No, they won't think that, either," Lentu contradicted. "Swain's horse bolted. You couldn't get his body on your horse an' take it down there alone, with your horse cuttin' up as he would be certain to do. Besides you was too shocked—see? All you thought of was getting back to the ranch an' tellin' what had happened. An' Swain's horse is probably almost there by now, so you'd better ride fast. You'll likely meet 'em comin' up to see what's happened."

"All right, I'll start back," said Neil, preparing to mount. "Won't the 3-X-Z bunch be liable to take after you fellows?"

"They'll never get a sight of us," Lentu promised earnestly. "Don't worry about that. We'll be gone, an' goin' fast; an' if we have any luck we'll have Left Hand in a tight place within forty-eight hours. Leave it to us. An', say, Sterret—"

Lentu stepped close to Neil. His eyes had narrowed and were unmistakingly cold and menacing.

"As I say, it would look bad for you if you was to mention us in this thing. Besides that, there's another reason why you better forget all about us when you begin to talk." Lentu's hand dropped like a flash of lightning to the butt of his gun. "It might not be healthy for you, understand? I'm your friend an' all that, but—*be careful!*"

The insinuation and the man's attitude were not lost upon Neil. He shuddered involuntarily as he nodded.

Lentu smiled grimly and stepped back as Neil mounted. "So long," he called softly.

As Neil urged his horse through the creek and went thundering down the trail, Lentu half drew his gun with a muttered oath. Then he vaulted into his saddle, motioned to his two companions who were waiting near by, and the three rode directly up the creek to a rocky and little-known trail that led into the higher mountains and far to the north around the plateau range to the ridge which joined the west shoulder of Angel Butte.

Neil, riding like mad down the Wild Horse trail, found his thoughts racing in keeping with the speed of his mount. Swain dead! Killed by Lentu! Had he really been trying to steal the cattle? Had it actually been a plan of Swain's and Left Hand's to rob his uncle? Had they known in advance that Amos Brodick was going to The Falls? Or was Lentu lying?

Again and again that question entered his mind. Was Lentu lying? Or— He actually checked his horse as a new theory presented itself. Had Lentu and his men been trying to run the herd off, and had Swain caught them in the act and been killed as a result? It seemed reasonably doubtful that Swain, a man who had worked for Amos Brodick for years, would deliber-ately plan to do such a thing at this time when, more than likely, he had had better opportunities in the past.

Neil's heart rose in his throat as he remembered the feud between the combine and his uncle. On the face of it what he had seen was in Swain's favor. He had been firing back over his shoulder; riding away from the cattle, not with them or ahead of them, as would have been the case if he had been driving them and had been taken unawares from behind. He had been fleeing back toward the ranch!

Lentu's first indecision now was explained. He had not expected to find Neil there, of course; had been nettled, in a quandary as to what to do. And then Neil's own question as to what Swain had been doing, and possibly some other silly questions he had asked in his excitement and speedily forgotten, had shown Lentu what course to take.

But there was the matter of Left Hand. Swain had shot the light out to help him. That was queer. And Left Hand had not ridden back to Angel Butte. Neil had heard some of the men from his uncle's ranch say that Left Hand had gone north. But even then—

No! Neil believed in his heart that Lentu was guilty.

Did he dare go back on his promise and tell all he knew? Lentu's parting words had virtually been a threat of death if he told all.

Neil felt that his hands were tied. He knew he could not bring himself to tell everything, for even as he thought of it he saw the cold, menacing, deadly gleam in Lentu's eyes as his hand had darted to the butt of his gun and he had made his threat.

It was with genuine terror that Neil rode around a bend in the trail above the head of the irrigation ditch and saw two men riding furiously toward him. His heart was in his mouth until he recognized Walt Frost and another man from the ranch. Swain's horse had carried the mute message of trouble to the 3-X-Z.

"Swain's been killed!" cried Neil as the two rode up.

"What's that you're sayin'?" asked Walt in astonishment. "Cool down a big, Sterret. What is it?"

And then Neil, terrified because of his situation, and a captive to his fears, told the story in breathless snatches just as Lentu had advised him. He had ridden up the valley to meet Swain, had gone on up to the plateau, had seen the cattle in the pass, had found Swain lying in the trail dead when he arrived there to learn what was the matter, and he had seen no one!

"Go back to the ranch," said Walt. "Tell Williams, he's acting foreman now. He sent us up to find out what had become of Swain. An' watch out for yourself on the way back."

In another moment Walt and the other were out of sight, riding madly up the creek trail.

Neil wiped the sweat from his face and hands. As Lentu had predicted, there had been no questioning of his story. And what, indeed, would his object have been in doing harm to Swain? It did seem ridiculous that any suspicion should be attached to him. More than likely there would be none. He was safe, unless—

Again came the vision of Lentu's sinister attitude at parting.

He was safe, and he would remain safe!

"Watch out for yourself on the way back," Walt Frost had said.

There was no need of that, Neil told himself bitterly. He rode on toward the ranch with his secret burning in his soul.

## CHAPTER XVIII
### THE UNEXPECTED MEETING

A T the ranch, Neil told the news, in a calm voice, although his face was pale under its tan, and his features were drawn and strained. Dora, catching the look of numbed horror in his eyes as he described the finding of Swain's body, felt sorry for him—and was drawn strangely toward him.

Mrs. French had made a light in the dining room, and it was there that Neil told his story to Williams, who, as assistant foreman, automatically stepped into the shoes of the dead man.

Williams listened intently, and by no word or action did he display any doubt of what Neil said. Even as he noted this fact, with secret relief and satisfaction, the youth also felt the queer pang within his breast. Did Williams suspect Swain's actions? Was that queer emotion which he felt within him a sense of loyalty to Swain? Whatever it was, Neil was glad when the ordeal was over and his account of the affair had been accepted at its word value.

"I will ride up to join Walt and Dan," said Williams after a thoughtful pause. "The cattle will be safe in the pass until tomorrow—with two men watching them. They can rest a day before we put 'em back on the range. I'll have the cook put up some grub for Walt an' Dan an' leave 'em up there—or, no, I'll stay up there myself an' send Dan down with the body. Neil, when you've had something to eat an' some sleep you ride down to Angel to meet your uncle when he comes in on the noon train from The Falls. Tell him what has happened. He will know what to do."

When Williams had left the room Dora went up to Neil. "Go and lie down, Neil," she said softly, "and when it is daylight I will call you, and we'll have a good breakfast ready for you to eat before you start for Angel."

As Neil looked at her he felt again that indefinable emotion within him. Was he—could it be that he was—ashamed? There was plenty of time yet to tell the whole story, he reasoned to himself. But he shuddered as he remembered Lentu and his threat: "It might not be healthy for you, understand?"

Neil understood.

Dora, mistaking the look in his eyes for one of compassion for the dead man or realistic awakening of his soul, put her hand gently upon his arm. "Go lie down, Neil," she urged. "You have a hard ride before you. Don't worry. Uncle will know what to do."

But Neil was worried. What would his uncle say? What would he do? What could he say or do? Neil, much fatigued and feeling the reaction from the excitement, dropped asleep, fully dressed, debating this in his mind.

When Dora woke him the dawn had come over the land. He ate his breakfast in silence and went out to find a fresh mount saddled and waiting for him at the gate. Sleep had done him a world of good, and now, as he rode over Angel Butte, his spirits revived in the fresh morning air, and he sighed with relief as he felt the strong, certain muscles of the horse beneath him.

He saw no sign of life, as with considerable apprehension, he passed the Double S ranch house. He did not know, naturally, that Lentu and Martin watched him from an upper window.

"He's goin' down to meet Amos," said Martin. "Now, Lentu, do you suppose—do you suppose—"

"Not a chance in the world," said Lentu, sneering. "He's kept his mouth shut. He's lucky, after dropping in the way he did. I didn't figure Swain would be up there, let alone that young brat!"

As Neil reached the last of the rolling slopes of the butte and swung into the nearly level stretch of prairie leading to Angel he saw the smoke-streamer left by a train drift along the horizon to the north. He spurred his mount to a last long spurt and arrived at the little railway station almost as the train was pulling in.

Covered with dust and breathing heavily, he confronted his uncle with his news as soon as Amos

131

Brodick stepped from the train.

Contrary to Neil's expectations, Brodick did not indulge in any exclamations, but stood looking dreamily out over the wide prairie to the west. Neil thought he saw something like a film shading his uncle's eyes; but the face of the old cattleman was grim and forbidding.

"I didn't reckon it would come so soon, Neil," said Amos finally. "Come—I must get back to the ranch." He saw Neil's horse standing covered with sweat. "Put him up in the New West barn," he instructed. "I'll go over an' get the horse Walt left here—he's fresh."

Amos Brodick swung up into the hotel stage as he finished speaking. Neil mounted and rode slowly to the barn. He told the man in charge to saddle the other horse and then met his uncle as he was coming out of the barn.

"Listen to me, Neil," said Amos Brodick. "There's a deputy sheriff in this town named Mills. I've asked for him, an' he's out in the country a ways, they tell me; but he's expected back soon. You stay here until he gets back and tell him about Swain. Tell him I asked for him to come out to the ranch, but not to make any fuss about it. He'll know what to do. Then you come home. An' don't do any talking."

Neil promised to carry out the orders. His uncle got his horse and started for the ranch.

Late that afternoon the deputy sheriff returned to Angel, and Neil met him on the porch of the hotel. The officer received the news much the same as Amos

Brodick heard it—without visible emotion or more than ordinary interest. This coincidence impressed Neil. Was life, then, held so cheaply in this new country?

"I shall have to do some work before I leave here, tell your uncle," said Mills. "I'll try to get up there tonight."

That was all the deputy said as he moved quickly away. Somehow Neil had felt that when the news was conveyed to the proper authorities it would be the signal for immediate action—the sending out of a posse, perhaps. But, apparently, Swain's death was causing not even a ripple in the official life of the county. It met with seemingly stoic indifference. It was almost as if it had been expected!

Yet all this gave Neil an increased feeling of security. His story so far had been accepted without question. Very likely he would not even be asked to repeat it. There was little danger of his having to incur the vengeful enmity of Lentu in an effort to ward suspicion from himself. His secret and his life were safe!

And yet, with this satisfying knowledge came a new sense of responsibility which was puzzling to Neil. He considered this as he rode out of Angel in the hour preceding the sunset. For the first time he felt himself a factor in the strange tangle of events which had transpired since he and Dora had come to the ranch.

He awoke suddenly to the realization that the feud between the combine and his uncle was a matter of life and blood. Lentu had said they were fighting for the open range, standing at the frontier to prevent its corruption by fool-headed farmers or would-be farmers who knew nothing of the country or its customs. He had painted a vivid picture of stirring scenes and wild range life that would come back into its own if the combine won—pictures that appealed to Neil's imagination, that thrilled and enthralled him. He had insisted that Neil's uncle would in time "wake up" and come to see things the combine's way, and that Neil would have an honored place in the activities of the victors when all the things he promised should come to pass. And he had taken sides against Left Hand, whom Neil hated, and against whom he felt utterly at a disadvantage. It was as if Neil had the deadly speed and accuracy of Lentu's gun between him and Left Hand in what he construed as his fight to keep Dora. Yes, it was better to have Lentu's gun for him than against him.

Nevertheless, the killing of Swain had served to impress Neil with the seriousness of the situation. His uncle against the combine! Again he felt that peculiar inner emotion which he did not understand. It seemed as if a new and strange trend of ideas were endeavoring to break through the barrier of argument built by Lentu—a barrier the Double S foreman was prepared to maintain by force.

When Neil's horse topped the last but one of the long, rolling slopes on the northern side of Angel Butte, the sunset was dying in the skies over the high mountains westward, and long banners of crimson and gold, slowly fading into the hazy purple of the twi-light, hung athwart the heavens. Neil halted to view the scene, fascinated by its beauty and its hint of infi-nite spaces.

Gradually his gaze became fixed on a swiftly moving, golden cloud of dust that whirled toward him along the grassy slope, and he soon made out a rider following a dry cattle trail which once had marked the thundering progress of the buffalo herds but now resounded to the dull, methodical pound of a horse's hoofs.

Closer and closer came the rider ahead of this swirling dust cloud, and Neil, thinking to avoid him as a sensible precaution, drove the spurs into his own mount. But the rider cut across, up the slope, and gained the trail a bit ahead, where he waited until Neil arrived.

Neil started in surprise not unmixed with apprehen-sion when he recognized the rider silently sitting his sweating, steaming horse in the trail, covered with dust which showed plainly in matted layers against his black chaps and shirt and high-crowned hat. His left side was toward Neil, and the youth saw the big, black butt of the gun which snuggled tight against the man's side, and caught the gleam of the sunset's fading fires on the cartridges in his belt.

It was Left Hand, arriving back at Angel Butte after a long, hard ride.

In a flash Neil remembered Lentu's hint that this man might have been involved with Swain in an attempt to steal his uncle's cattle. Had Lentu and his companions found the man at an appointed rendezvous waiting for Swain, and chased him?

"Just getting back from the celebration?" greeted Left Hand amiably as Neil's horse stopped.

"An' what if I am?" demanded Neil, emboldened by the other's apparent lack of hostility.

Left Hand's smile departed instantly. "Has your uncle got back to the ranch?" he asked coldly.

"My uncle's at the ranch, of course," replied Neil.

"Anything happened up your way?" asked Left Hand sharply.

Neil couldn't resist the impulse to answer: "Maybe you know as much about it as I do!"

"What is it?" snapped Left Hand.

"I don't know why I should be answering—"

"What has happened?" Left Hand interrupted. "Come, speak up—quick!" The man's left hand darted downward to his pistol, and his eyes flashed dangerously. "Speak up!"

"Swain's been killed," answered Neil, his face paling.

"Swain!" said Left Hand softly. For a moment he appeared deep in reflection. Then he looked at Neil somewhat curiously. "Let me give you a tip, young fellow," he said coldly. "Stay away from Lentu and his crowd. Show some sense. An' if I was you, I'd leave that gun at home." He drove in his spurs and rode swiftly down the trail, leaving Neil mad with futile anger.

As Neil started on up the trail he thought he heard an oath and a laugh borne back upon the breeze from the disappearing horseman. Once more his hatred of Left Hand aroused his suspicions as he hastened over the shoulder of the butte and turned down toward the ranch.

# CHAPTER XIX
## A GRAVE CONJECTURE

WHEN Neil arrived at the ranch he found that Swain's body had been brought down from the pass in the mountains, and that plans had been made to bury it next day. The men had made a coffin from available lumber stored in the hayloft of the horse barn, and in short shifts they watched over the body.

Deputy Mills arrived at the ranch that night, and to him Neil repeated his story in the presence of his uncle and Williams, the new foreman, and Walt Frost. Williams and Frost testified that an examination had revealed the fact that Swain had been shot twice *in the back*.

The officer put a few perfunctory questions to Neil, but neither he nor Amos Brodick nor any of the others seemed openly to doubt for a minute that Neil had told the truth and the whole truth.

Whatever surmises Amos Brodick might have indulged in, he did not put into words. He was strangely silent and grim. The officer stayed at the ranch that night and remained alone with Amos Brodick in the dining room until a late hour. He departed early in the morning.

Swain was buried the next day. The men stood around the coffin and the open grave while Amos Brodick read a burial service. Mrs. French and Dora, silent and fearful and with tears in their eyes, were present. When Amos had finished with the service the coffin was lowered into the grave, which had been dug in the lower slope of the butte above the pasture north of the house, and inclosed in a special fence. It was in a spot where the sun would almost always shine, except in bad weather, and where, according to the men, "Swain would have liked to lie if he could have chosen the place himself."

After the burial the various activities of the ranch became normal again. July slipped away without disturbance of any kind. The beef herd had been put back on the plateau at the head of Wild Horse Creek, but two men now were constantly on guard. It was planned to move these cattle down the creek in the early part of August and to graze them on the way, for Amos Brodick had the prior right, from the forest service, to most of the grazing land along the creek.

The north shoulder of Telltale Peak, which joined with the ridge that flattened out into the plateau where the beef herd was grazing, could be seen from the ranch. It had been arranged that in event of trouble on the plateau the men stationed there were to make a smoke signal on the north shoulder of Telltale Peak, and assistance from the ranch would be dispatched immediately.

All the men—and the women, too—had been carefully instructed by Amos Brodick to be alert for the sign of this smoke signal, and to report it to him at once if it should be seen. A fire in the same spot was to be the signal at night.

Now there was a lookout constantly on watch during the night. The men arranged these lookouts among themselves, and the duty never was neglected.

Aside from these precautions, the regular work of the ranch was carried on in the regular way. Neil had his duties and performed them willingly. In fact he had a genuine desire to learn as much as possible about ranch life and work. And his uncle, evidently desirous that he should learn the business from the ground up, as the saying has it, accorded him the same tasks—in so far as his experience would permit—and subjected him to the same discipline as the other men. He received his orders from Williams, and the new foreman could find no fault with the way in which he obeyed them. The men were quick to enlighten him when the occasion demanded and, for the most part, treated him as one of them, despite the fact that he slept in the house and ate his meals at the ranch-house dining table. He looked better than when he had arrived, too, and he had gained strength with his coating of healthy tan.

Neil studiously avoided thrusting his attention on

Dora, and he saw that this attitude on his part, and his steady application to his work, were effectively pleading his cause with her. Her pleasure frequently showed in her eyes when he would come in to supper tired and hungry and smile wistfully at her. But he was too shrewd to attempt to go further than the smile—as yet.

Amos Brodick, busy with the many affairs of the ranch, found but little time in which to pay any attention to the peculiar situation which existed between his nephew and Dora. Indeed the rancher seemed at times to be enjoying the little drama being played before his eyes and under his patronage.

"He's coming along all right," he said to Dora one evening when she had pressed him very subtly for an opinion as to Neil. "I think maybe along about Christmas time you two—" And then he broke out into a hearty laugh as Dora, blushing, left him alone on the porch.

But Neil, although he never voiced his thoughts, rather resented the fact that his uncle did not see fit to confide in him concerning his affairs. Amos Brodick, busy from early dawn until late at night, was accustomed to sit alone in his little office in the front of the house after he had finished for the day. Sometimes Neil detected a worried look in his uncle's eyes, and often he caught him standing musing with that expression which signified that his thoughts were many miles away.

Only once during these weeks of the glorious

summer of the foothills, with their blending of the heat of the prairie lands and the cool, pine-scented breezes of the higher ridges, did he make so bold as to interrupt his uncle's thoughts at night with a reference to the feud, as it now was generally called.

"Lentu and some of those others claim they can keep the homesteaders out up here just like they say they've kept the sheep out," Neil had said, supplementing his remark.

His uncle's eyes had flashed. "They can't seem to see that what they're tryin' to do is just the same as tryin' to stop the tide from coming up with a shingle. They can't stop it. An' sooner or later they're goin' to have it hammered into them—or shot into them—that folks are thinkin' different about the matter of the law now than they did—well, some years ago."

This was as much as Neil had been able to get out of his uncle with regard to the combine. And Neil couldn't help but contemplate in sheer astonishment the quiet manner in which the death of Swain had been received. There had been no attempt so far as he knew at investigation. The incident appeared closed with the lowering of the dead foreman's body into the grave and the taking of precautions to prevent another such tragedy.

It was then that a strange, awesome thought came to Neil, but he refused to give it credence. Still it recurred to him many times during the weeks after Swain's death, and it caused him to see his uncle in a new light—an uncomfortable light. He strove

141

earnestly to put the thought aside. It was merely conjecture, surely.

But from Dora, during their occasional talks, he learned more than from his uncle. It was from her he heard what Martin had said on the morning of the celebration in Angel. He decried the possibility of Left Hand being a gunman hired by his uncle, and agreed with Dora that this could not be true. Yet it set him thinking and again brought up the disagreeable conjecture.

From Dora, too, he heard the story of the Sand Creek hanging, which but served to add a new, sinister aspect to Lentu's unsavory reputation and attest to his viciousness.

Dora sought to convince him of the ruthlessness of this enemy of Amos Brodick. "Just think of such a man!" she cried. "A man who would deliberately murder two men under a flag of truce and drive a young boy out upon the prairie alone to die!"

This but served to convince Neil the more that his course in following Lentu's instructions regarding the story of Swain's death had been logical.

"And so you see," Dora had continued, "whatever can be said, it does look as though Left Hand was on our side since he is against Lentu and Martin and the others."

There it was again. Neil ground his teeth in ill-concealed rage. Why did Dora persist in sticking up for Left Hand? She had not forgotten the man, then. In Neil's mind Lentu's hatred for Left Hand compromised his undeniably bad qualities.

Left Hand a hired gunman of his uncle? Neil did not believe it. If such were indeed the case, why wasn't he on the ranch and close at hand? And if it were true, was it also true that Neil's conjecture was correct?

For the first time he deliberately asked himself the question: Was his uncle afraid?

Could this be the reason why little or nothing had been done about Swain's death?

Neil, mentally debating the matter from all angles, was compelled to conclude that everything pointed to his conjecture being the truth.

And then, one day late in July, Walt Frost returned from Angel with a load of supplies and some astonishing news.

"Left Hand has filed on the north of twenty-two and is building a shack there!" was his startling announcement.

The gunman had thrown the combine's defy of a deadline for homesteaders into its teeth and was boldly and openly taking possession of the forbidden ground!

# CHAPTER XX
## THE MIDNIGHT VIGIL

THE news of Left Hand's surprising move was the subject of exhaustive speculation among the men on the ranch, with the exception of Amos Brodick, who showed neither great surprise nor visible interest. His only cognizance of the new and amazing turn in affairs was to repeat his admonition to the men to be constantly alert in the event of a signal from Telltale Peak, which would announce a second attempt to rustle his cattle.

Neil, convinced that it was some kind of trick on the part of Left Hand, succeeded in sowing seeds of suspicion against him in an insidious way. He told of his meeting the man as he returned to the vicinity of the butte from a long, hard ride; intimated in a subtle way that Left Hand might know something of Swain's death, because Neil was not convinced for a certainty that the theft of the cattle was not a plan of Swain's and the gunman's.

Neil now saw his uncle in a new and depreciative light. He actually believed that Amos Brodick stood in deadly fear of Martin, Lentu, and the others of the combine!

"But, Neil, there is as much reason why Left Hand should file on a piece of land as anybody else," Dora had argued, when Neil had hinted at the way he felt about the whole matter.

"He could have filed when he first came here," Neil had retorted. "And if he's wanted by the authorities as they say, he had to file under some name besides his own—whatever it is—and he couldn't very well except to keep and prove up a homestead under an assumed name."

Meanwhile the whole ranch watched for the fulfilling of the combine's threat against any one who should dare to file inside of the dead line laid down in the spring.

The combine's guards had been withdrawn, it was learned. Possibly they didn't want to clash with Left Hand. But it was generally believed that the combine had assumed that its threat had made good and had not expected a filing on twenty-two.

During July the newly erected shacks of the homesteaders had crept steadily westward from the town of Angel; now they had reached the eastern flanks of the butte, although they had not encroached upon the north side, where there was a vast expanse of range still used by the combine as grazing land for its cattle.

There was one shack in this territory now, however. It was the shack which Left Hand had built in a day after he had had the rough lumber hauled out from Angel, and had sat beside the driver, gun in hand and with a rifle behind him, to answer any leaden messengers of protest which the combine might speed in his direction.

But there had been no show of hostility while the shack was being built. Peace and quiet reigned upon the butte, which reared its majestic bulk against a clear blue field of sky, brilliant with sunshine, glowing in gold and green, topped with spires of limestone that gleamed with the whiteness of marble.

Dora had found a trail which wound around the east side of the butte to its crest, and on several afternoons when she had been riding she had followed this trail to the summit, to gaze out upon the far-flung scene of prairie grandeur with its background of purple mountains—the Rockies, the Big and Little Belts, and, in the southeast, the Highwoods.

On the afternoon following the announcement that Left Hand had filed on twenty-two and was building a shack there, she rode again up the winding trail to the top of the butte. On her first trip, weeks before, she had seen a glimmer of Left Hand's camp through the pine growth midway of the descent of the east side of the butte. But the camp had disappeared. Left Hand had moved to some other section of that side of the butte, possibly down by the deep sluice boxes cut in the limestone near the foot of the butte, where the waters of Band Creek, augmented by those of Wild Horse Creek, surged on their way to join the mighty Missouri.

This afternoon the girl viewed with a thrill the little structure of rough boards which stood alone far down the north slope, a tangible, visible, saucy-appearing defy to the combine. Forlorn, insignificant as it would have looked to a stranger in the locality, Dora knew, nevertheless, that it portended something mighty in the lives of those who lived around the butte. The very stillness of the air and peaceful beauty of the scene held a note of sinister foreboding—as of a wild animal asleep before the hunt.

Sitting on a boulder in the shade of some gnarled and wind-twisted pines, Dora lost track of the passage of time and was suddenly brought to her senses by the soft shading of the light and the delicate rose tints of the skies, which proclaimed the sunset.

Hurriedly she rose and went for her horse, grazing in a meadow a short way down the slope. As she prepared to mount she heard the rattle of stones upon the rocky trail. In another moment, while she hesitated in wonder and with a vague feeling of alarm, Left Hand came into view riding up the trail, and pulled in his horse close to her.

He shook his head slowly and scowled.

Although Dora had heard many stories which tended to stamp this man as a dangerous, ruthless character, she found that she was not afraid of him—had never been afraid of him. Neither did she find herself considering him in the same light as she considered Lentu, another gunman and reputed killer. Although she could not reason exactly what it was which convinced her, she felt that there was a difference between the two men, even though they might each be deserving of the reputations bestowed upon them.

Left Hand continued to shake his head as he looked at her. The scowl quickly faded, however. "You shouldn't be doing this," he said finally in a tone of reproval. "It isn't exactly safe."

"What have you reference to, Mr. Left Hand?" asked Dora with a tilt of her head.

"You shouldn't come up on this butte—not these days," replied the man.

"If that is what you think, you will be kind enough to tell me why," she retorted.

"Because there are dangerous men around here, and while maybe you don't understand, it isn't altogether safe for you to go so far away from the ranch, ma'am—up here especially."

"If I am to believe all I hear you are one of the dangerous men, Left Hand," she said, gazing at him keenly. She noted that his eyes looked troubled, and his face was grim; he had forgotten to remove his hat.

"Perhaps," he replied quickly and, she thought, whimsically. "But you have nothing to fear from me, ma'am."

"Of course not!" she exclaimed, but found herself at a loss for further words.

"It might not be the same with all the men up here," he went on. "An', besides, now that I've put that button on the landscape down there"—he pointed toward the lone shack in the north—"I'd like to have this place up here clear so I can keep an eye on it, an' there's others that might not like the idea of my being up here, an'—well, this ain't liable to be the healthiest spot around here, ma'am, if you know what I mean."

Dora knew what he was endeavoring to convey. She

mounted to obtain time in which to think, and decided upon a bold question.

"Left Hand, do you know what they—what some people are saying about you?" she asked.

This brought a short laugh. "I could manage a guess."

"I don't mean about your—your business," she said.

"My business?" he asked sharply. "What do they say is my business?"

Dora could not find the courage to tell him in so many words, but she nodded toward the gun strapped to his left thigh.

"Oh, that!" He smiled, and she thought he looked relieved.

"And they say you are in the employ of my uncle," she continued. "His—his gunman."

Again the short laugh. "And you want to know if that's true, eh, ma'am?"

"If I have the right to ask," she faltered. "I am not altogether familiar with customs out here, but—"

"Don't worry," he interrupted cheerfully. "You needn't have any fears 'bout me being in your uncle's pay. And in return for that information I wish you'd promise not to come up on the butte again—for a while, anyway."

She was about to reply to this when they were both startled by the approach of another rider. Left Hand whirled his horse and called to her over his shoulder to move away from behind him. His hand closed over the butt of his pistol as Neil came into view riding a sweating, nearly winded horse. Neil halted and stared at them with eyes which nearly popped from his head, and which flashed with anger.

"So this is the way it is!" he ejaculated with a sneer.

Dora urged her horse forward. "Neil, I came up here for the ride and the view, as I've often come, and Left Hand happened to find me here and——"

"Happened!" Neil cried.

Dora flushed at his tone and what it implied.

"That's what she said," put in Left Hand. "I happened upon her here an' told her it wasn't safe for her to be coming, if you want to know."

"Just giving her a little advice, I suppose," said Neil, sneering again.

"You got any objections?" queried Left Hand coolly.

"I suppose you're just hanging around here to give folks advice—women especially," said Neil, now white-faced with anger.

"You could take a little advice yourself without its hurting you none," Left Hand observed. "An' what I was telling the lady was on the square—about her coming up here."

"I want you to understand," Neil flared, "that the lady you're talking about is my wife!"

"Neil, you don't understand," Dora implored.

"I understand that this fellow is meddling with somebody else's wife," said Neil viciously.

"My advice to you," drawled Left Hand, "is to try an' be worthy of your wife an' not be a—coyote!"

With a veritable scream of rage Neil's hand dropped

to the butt of his gun, but the calm, forbidding look in the other man's eyes arrested his movement. Instinctively he knew that he had not one chance in a thousand of drawing his weapon before the other could get his gun into action.

"Don't do it, my boy, don't try it," cautioned Left Hand. "And don't get any fool ideas into your head about this chance meeting of mine with your wife. She's telling you the truth. This is not a safe place for her at present, an' I came up here to tell her so. Take her back, for it'll be dark before long. An' remember what I said about the—coyote."

Dora guided her horse ahead of Neil's and began the descent. "Thank you," she called back to Left Hand.

"Don't mention it, ma'am," returned the gunman.

Neil, tortured by futile rage, turned his horse. "The odds are on your side," he called back to Left Hand. "They're on your side—this time."

"I aim to have 'em that way most of the time," said Left Hand coldly, as he watched the riders disappear.

"I guess it's a good thing I happened to see you striking up this trail," Neil called to Dora after a time.

"Don't talk to me, Neil," Dora cried with tears welling in her eyes. "Don't speak to me—now."

Back on the summit of the butte Left Hand tied his horse in a thick clump of trees under the lee of a huge outcropping of limestone. He went to the north end of the rocky ridge on the crest of the butte and, after a long, searching gaze at the wide panorama below him, rolled and lit a cigarette and began to pace slowly back and forth along the rim, where he was in the shadow of the twisted pines, but had an unrestricted view.

Slowly the crimson banners of sunset shaded to gold and blue in the west, and the soft, hazy, purple veil of the twilight drew across the land and gradually deepened into night—the clear, cool night of the foothills, with the darkened vault of the heavens alive with stars.

At the coming of the dusk a faint light showed in the single window of the little shack—the window on the south side toward the butte. As night descended the light shone brighter and brighter until it, too, appeared like a star—a star fallen to rest against the velvet-black background of prairie.

Left Hand watched it with eyes agleam as he paced the rim of the summit. His features were tense; his attitude that of impatience, but not indecision. He was biding his time.

"If that lamp'll just hold out long enough," he muttered to himself, "maybe it'll attract attention."

He kept his gaze roving toward the dark slope in the direction of the Double S. Now and then he would walk nearly around the crest of the butte to west and south, where he would pause and stare whimsically in the direction of the Brodick ranch, and then quickly retrace his steps to the north rim of the summit.

"His wife," he said softly to himself. "An' she asking me one day what the West did to a man. An' him, blind as a bat, actin' like a danged coyote!"

The moon, which had appeared with the coming of night, sank closer and closer to the mountain tops. There it seemed to hang just above the peaks and then slip quickly behind them. The darkness deepened. Still the light shone in the window of the little shack below—a blazing symbol of defiance.

Left Hand's watch showed the hour of midnight as he scanned its face in the flickering light of a match behind the shelter of the rocks where his horse was tethered.

Now he kept his gaze fixed on the long, black slope which led to the west shoulder of the butte and the Double S. An hour passed. He looked down toward the light. It had dimmed as if it were going out, or as if it had been turned low.

"Just as I figured," he said to himself, then suddenly straightened and strained his eyes toward the Double S. At the upper end of the slope he saw a shadow—a blotch of ill-defined darkness against the background of the slope barely discernible in the pale glow of the stars. Again he saw it, and then it blended with the blackness farther down the slope.

Left Hand hurried to his horse, untied him, and led him down the trail and around through the pine growth to the north side of the butte. Mounting, he descended swiftly in the cover of the sparse timber until he reached its lower fringe. Here he tied his horse again and then began to creep silently and stealthily down the slope.

There were now two blotches of darkness, two

vague forms stealing down the slope toward the dim
light in the shack window.

# CHAPTER XXI
## A SINISTER PROPHECY

THE night wind breathed in the prairie wastes as the
two shadows glided toward the shack. One
moved quickly down from the southwest slope; the
other cut across from the fringe of timber, moving
slowly and pausing at regular intervals, keeping close
to the ground in order to blend with the blackness of
the plain.

When the first shadow reached the shack it crept
slowly to the window, and gradually the outlines of a
man's head and shoulders stood out against the faint
glow of the dimming lamp within. The second shadow
moved rapidly but silently now. And when the man
before the window, having satisfied himself that there
was no one inside, turned quickly to look about him,
he found himself staring into the bore of a six-shooter
held in a steady hand. Slowly his stare traveled from
the gun to the face above it; became fixed upon the
eyes which transfixed his. His hands went high above
his head.

Without speaking Left Hand stepped forward and
possessed himself of Lentu's gun. He motioned with
his pistol toward the front of the shack, and Lentu
moved around to the door, still keeping his hands ele-

vated. Left Hand opened the door and followed Lentu inside. He lit another lamp upon the table and put out the one which was smoking and empty.

"I sort of expected you'd call," said Left Hand. "I fixed that light on purpose so you'd think it was an invitation. Sit down, but put your hands on the table!"

Lentu obeyed the commands. "I didn't know but what that light was a blind," he said surlily. "I don't care if it was. I came down here to see you."

Left Hand dropped into the other chair by the table, a corner of which separated him from Lentu. He stared at Lentu with a directness which momentarily nonplused the other. There was an undefinable but easily distinguishable gleam of hatred and gloating in that stare—an undubitable menace, absolutely sincere.

"I say I came down here on purpose to see you," Lentu repeated.

"Yes?" Left Hand seemed to lisp the word so that it carried something of a hiss as it left his lips.

"Oh, I intended to get the drop on you if I could," Lentu said with a smirk, and the grimace he intended for a grin seemed strangely out of place. "But that's as far as I had intended to go—tonight."

Left Hand laughed. Lentu thought he detected a note in the laugh which made it seem more sinister than the other's continued, disconcerting starc.

"What did you want to talk to me about?" asked Left Hand coolly. "I mean, what did you think you wanted to talk to me about? Or, did you have to have the drop on me to talk?"

Lentu wet his lips. His eyes had narrowed. He was not a coward. But there was something in the cold, almost fiendish gleam of the eyes which looked into his own that gave him a new sensation. He did not try to grin again.

"I'm asking you what you wanted to talk to me about," Left Hand reminded him sharply.

"Why, it's just this—it's—well, Left Hand, I don't know what your game is, but, whatever it is, why couldn't it be played better on our side?"

In the silence which ensued, the gentle drone of the prairie wind could be heard. This sound was quickly drowned in a harsh, mirthless laugh from Left Hand— a laugh that sent a chill into the very marrow of Lentu's bones. It was almost like the laugh of a madman. Indeed, it seemed to suggest downright savage joy.

"Lentu, you're a fool," said Left Hand grimly.

"You might get more from us than from old Brodick," said Lentu.

"I'll get all I want from you!" cried Left Hand.

Again Lentu felt the strange sensation, the chill. He avoided that stare. Could it be that the unknown thing he felt was fear? Was he to be shot down in cold blood?

"So you came here with a proposition?" Left Hand said suavely. "Because I've crossed your dead line an' planted a shack on twenty-two? Because you think I'm working for Brodick?"

"Because we could use you," retorted Lentu, and he probably spoke the truth.

Left Hand leaned on the table. His eyes were glowing with a strange, fierce gleam. "How do you know I ain't working for myself?" he asked.

"A gunman like you don't deliberately butt into anybody's play unless there's something in it for him, does he?" countered Lentu. "I know your reputation——"

"But do you know me?" demanded the other sharply.

Looking straight into the burning eyes before him, Lentu felt the same thrill which had crept over him when he had confronted the man in the saloon at Angel the night of the celebration. The sweat stood out upon his forehead in glistening beads while his mind tugged vainly at the strings of memory. And, as he met the other's stare, he knew the look would mean but one thing—death. Left Hand intended to kill him! He glanced swiftly about him, and as he glanced Left Hand smiled; his face seemed to light with joy and satisfaction—with triumph.

"No chance," he said softly; "not a chance. Lentu, you—haven't—got—a—chance! Don't you see I'm sitting here gloating over you? That's what I'm doing—gloating! And yet you're sure goin' out of this shack alive! I'm goin' to let you go just like a cat lets a mouse go—an' then catches it again—an' kills it! If you could only think maybe you wouldn't get out of here so easy. But you can't think—yet. You're right. I'm workin' for somebody. That's why I've got to let you go. Now, ain't that strange?"

Left Hand laughed, but the other didn't join him in his mirthless hilarity.

"You say you know my reputation, Lentu? Well, I want you to be sure—*sure*, understand? Do you remember the night we met in Angel? I always wondered why you didn't draw that night, Lentu. You didn't make a move until you thought you had the advantage. An' now we're here alone in this shack, an' you're wishing you had your gun that I threw in the corner. Lentu, do you see that knot in that middle board of the door?"

Left Hand's voice seemed to purr as he pointed to the knot midway the height of the door.

"Now that ain't such a big knot, Lentu; it's a lot smaller than a man's heart—a right small mark, to get down to cases. Now you watch!"

Left Hand slipped his gun into the sheath of his left side, and rose to a half crouch. "Now, Lentu, hold up your right forefinger. Don't worry, I'm not goin' to shoot it off, nor shoot you. You don't know why, but you're as safe here with me tonight as if you was tucked in your own bed. All I want you to do is crook that finger now that you've got it up there."

Lentu hesitated. But, looking into the man's eyes in the glow of the light from the lamp, he realized that Left Hand meant just what he said. Lentu's eyes glittered. The fool was actually going to give an exhibition of his speed with his gun. Deliberately going to give him a chance to view him in action; to compare his speed with his own—Lentu's. It was like exposing one's hand at poker and then going on with the game. It might give Lentu an advantage in a future meeting. Was the man a supreme egotist? Was he overplaying his hand? For the first time Lentu smiled naturally as he crooked the finger.

But the smile died cold on his lips. It seemed to him as if he had hardly moved his finger—just decided to move it—when the left hand of the man before him moved faster than the eye could follow, and the sharp thunder of the gun shattered the death-like stillness.

Lentu's eyes popped in amazement at the magical, lightning swiftness of the draw he had witnessed. Slowly his fascinated gaze shifted from the weapon at Left Hand's hip to the knot in the door. It was punctured almost directly in the center!

"You see!" cried Left Hand gayly. "Did you see?"

Lentu remained silent. He had seen fast work with a gun; had had to beat some fast men. But never had he witnessed such speed as Left Hand had exhibited. What was the object? Coolly he appraised the other as he sat down and again leaned upon the table. And then the question formed in Lentu's mind—shone in his eyes. Could he, Lentu, draw and shoot as fast as that?

It was as if Left Hand could read his very thought. His eyes burned into Lentu's with deadly seriousness, and his lips tightened as he slowly shook his head with an earnest conviction.

"You ain't got a chance, Lentu; that's what I want you to remember. That's the way I want it—when the time comes. That little show I staged wasn't a bluff." Left Hand pointed to the bullet hole in the knot in the board of the door. "I wanted you to see; I wanted you to know. You won't have a chance!"

Lentu's face turned a purplish red with anger. Was the man trying to scare him—to frighten him out of an encounter which he predicted?

"I ain't got a chance now," he said, openly sneering.

"An' you didn't have one down in Angel, though you didn't know it. An' you won't have one the next time. A man always gets what's coming to him, Lentu."

"So you're a preacher as well as a gun fighter," said Lentu as he sneered again.

"Not a preacher, Lentu! I'm a prophet!"

Left Hand walked to the corner where he had thrown the other's weapon. He picked it up, broke it, spilled the shells on the floor, handed it to Lentu, and motioned toward the door. As Lentu went out Left Hand extinguished the light and followed him up the long slope, but when Lentu reached the top and turned around, he was alone.

# CHAPTER XXII
## A TRIANGLE

THE following day Neil, outwardly cool and composed and reserved in his attitude toward Dora, inwardly raged in bitterness toward Left Hand. The fact that he believed Dora's statement that she had merely ridden to the top of the butte for the exercise and the view did not alter his conviction that the man had followed her there—that he was deliberately soliciting her favor; and her look of reproval at breakfast merely caused the tumult in his thoughts to flare the more ominously.

After breakfast Amos Brodick instructed Neil to ride to Angel with some letters for the post. These had to do, he said, with the prospective sale of the beef cattle, which were to be brought down from the plateau range within a week—as soon as the alfalfa hay had been put up.

On the ride to Angel, Neil kept a sharp lookout for sight of Left Hand, but his vigil was unrewarded. He saw no one in the vicinity of the Double S, either. He stared darkly at the shack on the north half of section twenty-two, erected, as he knew, by Left Hand, but to all outward appearances deserted.

"Builds a shack and then hides in the timber," growled Neil savagely as he drove in his spurs and hastened toward the prairie town of Angel far below.

It was still some time until noon when Neil rode into

the town and went directly to the general store, which contained the post office. After posting his uncle's letters he took the horse to the hotel barn to be rested, watered, and fed against his return. Then he sauntered around to the front of the hotel and the main street. He was in an ugly mood, and this mood was not improved by his reflection that he could think of no way in which to get even—as he thought the case required—with Left Hand.

In this frame of mind he entered the Prairie Flower saloon. It was the first time he had been in the place since the memorable night when he had participated in the blackjack game and incurred the displeasure of the dealer, Ratty.

Almost as soon as he walked in through the door he caught sight of the dealer. He walked to the bar and called for a drink—such as was sold openly. The strenuous nature of Neil's thoughts gave him a courage and aggressive appearance which was far different from the impression he had made on that night some two months before. In addition, he felt a dawning confidence in himself.

Watching in the mirror behind the bar he saw the dealer looking at him curiously and apparently disdainfully. This nettled him and aggravated his temper, which already was raw. Only a few were gathered around the table where the game was in progress, as it nearly always was in progress both day or night.

As Neil finished his drink—the only one he

intended to take that day, he told himself—he was surprised to see Lentu enter hurriedly by the back door, which was open, and signal to two men in cowpuncher garb who were standing near the table watching the game. Lentu spoke to the men a moment, and then the two went out of the rear door. Neil assumed that they were employees of the combine.

Lentu seemed surprised to see him there when he came to the bar. He insisted that Neil drink with him, and Neil, finding that the liquor—a special brand which a wink from Lentu brought forth—fanned the flame of his angry passion and, becoming more vengeful in his thoughts, told the Double S foreman of the encounter with Left Hand the evening before, and of his suspicions. Lentu's eyes glistened as he paid marked attention to Neil's words and then deftly ascertained that Neil had concealed the most important phase of the incident of Swain's death in the story he had told his uncle and the others. He appeared satisfied. He said nothing to Neil of his extraordinary session of the night before with Left Hand in the shack on the north slope of Angel Butte.

A bell sounded from a restaurant next to the saloon, and most of the men around the gaming table left to get dinner. Ratty closed the game temporarily, and when his boosters went out to eat he crossed over to the bar.

He stood at the lower end between Neil and the door, at Neil's left. Lentu stood at Neil's right and nudged Neil's arm as Ratty came up to the bar. "He's got more respect for you than he used to have," said Lentu in an undertone.

The remark pleased Neil, who leaned against the bar with a swaggering, confident air.

But Ratty's forthcoming remark did not seem to indicate any great degree of newly acquired respect. "I see you've added chaps an' spurs to the hat," he said with the suggestion of a sneer.

Neil's eyes glittered and narrowed in surprise and anger, Lentu glanced significantly at the bartender.

"Did you ever stop to think that you've got as much as you can tend to if you look after your own business?" retorted Neil.

"I'm capable of doin' that, young feller," said Ratty.

"He's bluffing," Lentu whispered to Neil with hardly a movement of his lips. "He's scared of you, an' is tryin' to cover it up. I know him like a book— the coyote."

At the word coyote Neil bristled. Left Hand had used that word in connection with himself the evening before. At the very thought of it Neil's anger rose again. Here was another enemy who had humiliated him, present in the flesh to receive the brunt of his rage. Ratty did not look very dangerous, and Neil had the spur of his wrathful thoughts to drive him on.

"An' what's that hanging on his side?" Ratty snickered as he put down his glass. "Why, darn my stars if he ain't gone to packing a gun!"

Neil's eyes blazed with fury.

"What you totin' that aroun' for, son?" Ratty taunted

164

with a wink at Lentu. "Do you see how quick they get to be bad men when they come out here from the East?" he asked the bartender.

"Pull your gun an' send a couple of shots over his head," whispered Lentu excitedly. "He'll run like a scared rabbit. He ain't armed, anyway. Hurry up. Throw a scare into him!"

And Neil, approving the idea in a flash, and in the same instant recollecting that he had Lentu behind him, in any event, pulled his gun and fired twice over Ratty's head. The bartender dodged down behind the bar at the first move. It seemed to Neil that the second shot sounded considerably louder than the first. And then he looked at Ratty in unfeigned amazement as the dealer's body swayed back from the bar and toppled to the floor.

"Good Lord!" cried Lentu loudly, running to bend over the fallen man. "Great guns, Sterret," he gasped, "you've killed him!"

An icy chill of horror and fear struck at Neil's heart as he stood and stared down at the body of the dead dealer and then looked open-mouthed at his gun.

"Put that gun up, quick," snapped Lentu, as he turned the body over and withdrew a snub-nosed revolver from one of the dead man's hip pockets. "Ratty just couldn't draw fast enough for the kid," he explained to the bartender as the man came slowly from his hiding place. Lentu dropped Ratty's gun close to the stiffening fingers of the hand which stuck out from under the body.

"Sterret, get out that back door," commanded Lentu. "Get your horse an' get out of town as fast as you can ride—an' keep your mouth shut!"

Still Neil remained rooted to the spot with horror, unable to comprehend the tragedy which had befallen him in such an incredibly short space of time. The sweat burst out upon his face and forehead and hands as he returned his weapon to its sheath. There must be some mistake, he thought wildly—some kind of accident. He had shot high; he had not intended to—

"Hurry an' make your get-away, you fool," roared Lentu. "A posse might not stop to ask questions except with a rope. I'll head 'em off if I can. Are you going, or—"

Neil didn't wait to hear the rest of it but ran for the back door. As he leaped outside he turned for a fleeting glimpse over his shoulder and caught swift sight of Left Hand standing in the front doorway. For an instant he wavered, wondering; then he dashed for the hotel barn, got his horse, and rode like mad out of town in the direction of the butte.

Driving home his spurs with a cruel viciousness that made his horse snort with pain and extend itself to the utmost, Neil dashed across the open country to the bottom of the first of the series of long, easy slopes which led up and around the north side of the butte to its western shoulder and the cañon trail down to Wild Horse Creek.

Here Neil slacked his pace somewhat. What if he were followed? Wouldn't his pursuers go straight for the ranch and find him there? Then what? His distorted brain pictured a noose swinging from the limb of a tree and himself standing under it striving to explain what had happened to a posse of grim-faced men. What would he say? What could he say? He needed time to think, and above everything else he wanted to know if he was followed.

He looked quickly about him, and his gaze, as he checked his horse, centered upon the tumbled country to the south, below the eastern side of the butte, where Brand Creek wound through the sluice boxes cut in the soft limestone. There he could hide and watch!

Without further thought about the matter he turned his horse from the trail and rode rapidly south until he had gained the shelter of the bad lands, with their growth of cottonwoods and willows near the sluice boxes. He mounted to the top of a rise of ground and, after securing his horse among the trees on the west side, crawled to the edge of a limestone ledge on the east and fixed his gaze upon the open trail in the northeast, over which he had ridden from Angel.

He hardly had time to settle himself for his vigil before he saw a cloud of dust racing on the wind from the direction of the town. His heart swelled in his throat. A posse? Men, maddened and eager for vengeance, already upon his trail? With the thought Neil became strangely quiet and composed—clear-headed and able to think.

Speedily he realized that it was too small a dust cloud to be made by a body of horsemen, and this surmise soon proved to be correct; for he made out a single rider coming rapidly on the main trail to the butte. A few minutes later he recognized the form in the saddle as Lentu.

Neil was at first prompted to mount and ride out to the trail to meet the oncoming horseman. But before he could yield to this impulse he was stayed by another. He felt a wave of hot anger toward the Double S foreman. Lentu had told him to shoot. It was not Lentu's fault, perhaps, that he had followed the suggestion; but Lentu had been responsible for it, just the same.

Again Neil was struck with wonder at the result of his shots. He would have sworn at the last bar of judgment that he had aimed high, much higher than Ratty's head. He remembered that second shot; it had sounded louder than the first. Could it be that the cartridge was overloaded, and that the bullet had split, and part of it had gone low and killed Ratty? But he caught himself smiling; little as he knew about weapons and ammunition such a thing did not seem probable or possible. He decided that he would not ride out to meet Lentu; he watched as the Double S foreman disappeared around a bend on the first slope.

Thinking clearly now, Neil realized that the affair looked mighty bad for him. He had had trouble with Ratty. Doubtless every man who frequented the Prairie Flower saloon knew about the altercation which had taken place on the occasion of Neil's first visit there. He had not been in the place since—until this day. And on this second visit Ratty had been shot and killed by—but Neil could not bring himself to say, even in a whisper or in his thoughts, that he had committed the crime.

All the enmity he had felt toward Ratty had been blotted out by the feel and sound of the shots and the gruesome sight of the crumpled body on the floor. Neil hated heartily the very recollection of the bravado he had felt earlier in the day. He was not a killer, and he knew now what he had not known before—that he had no desire to be a killer, to take life.

Without looking at it, Neil drew out his gun, broke it, removed the empty shells, and flung them away from him in hearty disgust. He loathed the very feel of the pistol as he hurriedly slipped in two new shells and returned it to its sheath. He thought it would be best not to have two empty shells in the chamber.

He forgot it on the instant as he sighted another small dust cloud whirling above the trail out from town. An officer? He watched breathlessly as the rider approached and then uttered a startled cry of amazement and consternation.

The rider had left the main trail to Angel Butte and had cut off to the south. He rode for some distance directly south and then swung toward the west. Neil leaped to his feet and then crouched motionless on the very edge of the limestone in an agony of indecision.

The rider was coming in his direction! He was

coming fast. And, though Neil's every instinct urged him to flee, he remained as though rooted to the spot.

## CHAPTER XXIII
### THE SIGNAL

HIGH above the glistening rock dome of Telltale Peak at the head of the narrow valley wherein Wild Horse Creek nursed its waters, hung a mass of feathery clouds. They had been there the day before— a thin wisp of shadowy veil that had gathered form during the night. The cloud mass attested to the warrant for the tradition of the peak, which was that the appearance of this vapor banner high over its summit foretold a change in weather—a storm. Already the wind had gathered volume and was whistling across the ridges and down between the timbered slopes of the valley and over the prairie lands, from the west.

Lentu, arriving at the Double S on his lathered horse, found a number of men there waiting for him, including those he had sent out from Angel. He quickly changed his saddle to a fresh steed in the big corral and ordered the men to mount. Time and again, as he went about the business of changing horses, his gaze sought the sky above the ridges west of the ranch in the direction of Telltale Peak, which he could not see because of the nearness of an intervening rib of range which joined the west shoulder of Angel Butte.

"Did that young cub from Brodick's place ride past

here?" he demanded of one of the men.

"If he did he must have changed himself into a breath of wind," was the answer. "We ain't seen hide or hair of any rider but yourself an' the boys that came from town."

Lentu frowned but vouchsafed no comment. Vaulting into the saddle he led the men out upon the long, undulating north slope of the butte. Here he paused to make sure of the direction of the wind. The sear, dry, brown-gold grass of the prairie rippled in waves as the wind caressed it, shaping it momentarily into miniature windrows, smoothing it again, bending it, wrinkling it, flattening it, tossing it until the whole vast reach of the plain appeared to be trembling violently; and the motion always was toward the east, toward the single shack in the foreground on the north half of twenty-two, toward the other shacks which dotted the flatlands east of the slopes of the butte, toward the town of Angel with its rough-board structures and its board-floored tents, dry as tinder, highly inflammable, needing but a spark in the gathering force of the wind to become a caldron of flame and a fiery heap of smoldering embers.

Lentu spread his men in the shape of a fan, the farthest being two miles out across the slope, and he himself took up a position at a point near the trail on the west shoulder of the butte, where he awaited a favorable moment to give a prearranged signal. The men all had dismounted. Lentu slowly raised his hands, and for a moment they all bent low, then leaped back into their saddles and raced madly for the trail behind the Double S ranch house, which wound along the north slope of the western ridge toward the plateau near Telltale Peak, though there were a number of trails which surmounted the ridge and threaded thin paths through the timber to the valley of Wild Horse Creek.

It was Williams, the new foreman, who called Amos Brodick from his little front office in the 3-X-Z ranch house in the early afternoon.

"There's smoke on Telltale Peak, sir!"

Amos Brodick rose quickly from his desk and ran out upon the porch. Far at the head of the valley, its gleaming dome and the darker shadow of its right spur outlined against the skies, was Telltale; and curling from the right spur was a spiraling feather of smoke.

"Saddle my horse!" shouted Amos. "You and Walt Frost and one of the other men come with me. That's a signal from the men with the cattle."

The ranch was in a hubbub of excitement. Men were running from the fields and the garden toward the house. Williams waved them back, with the exception of one who was to accompany Frost, himself, and Amos Brodick.

"If you hear firing, or if we have not sent word or returned before morning, send the other men," Amos Brodick told Mrs. French. "Let's see. There'll be five left, an' when Neil gets back he'll make six. Keep Neil an' the cook an' another here, whatever happens. This may be Martin's work. It may just be trouble with the cattle. But we can't leave the ranch an' you women unprotected. I think maybe there'll be other help coming if it's serious."

The women watched white-faced as the four men galloped up the creek trail.

Amos Brodick's face was grim, and his eyes were burning with the fire of combat as he led the way up the valley, riding hard and keeping his gaze on the trail ahead and the smoke signal, which loomed above the right spur of Telltale. As they slowly neared the head of the valley, where the trail to the plateau cut through the timber and up the ridge to the right, the cattleman checked his horse with a startled exclamation, and pointed high to the left and straight ahead.

The men swore softly as they looked. In the timber under the lee of Telltale and farther down into the valley flickering tongues of red were licking at the dry underbrush and trees, and leaping high with showers of sparks where the wind caught them and fanned them as with some gigantic bellows.

"The forest is afire!" cried Amos as he spurred his mount. "That's what's the matter. The boys are having trouble gettin' the cattle out!"

Pushing their horses to their utmost speed the four men rode for the head of the valley and the trail to the plateau. Already the fires were climbing the slope toward the tableland, where were the cattle. If it reached the plateau it would sweep across it on the wind in an incredibly short time. The only trail from the flatland where the cattle were grazing, over which the stock could be driven safely out, was that which led down into Wild Horse Valley. If the fire should reach this trail before the cattle could be removed it would mean their extermination and would involve Amos Brodick in a loss from which he could recover only with extreme difficulty—if at all. Payments and interest were due upon his place, and he was depending upon the beef herd to tide him over the lean years which had followed his removal from the Teton country after the affair of the Sand Creek hanging.

As the horses plunged across the narrow strip of valley and began the climb to the plateau, one of the men who had been left in charge of the big herd appeared suddenly in the trail sitting his horse and holding up a hand, palm outward, as a signal for them to stop.

"What's the matter?" demanded Amos angrily. "Why ain't you tryin' to get the cattle out?"

"Because the minute a man's head shows on that plateau it's the target for shots from the timber," was the answer.

"Shots? Whose?" demanded Amos.

"That I don't know," the man replied. "It began about noon, when we first saw the smoke from the fires in Wild Horse Valley. When we started to round up the cattle an' drive 'em to the trail the bullets began to whistle through our hats. My other horse was shot dead under me. Several of the steers was hit by hot lead an' keeled over. Then we built the signal fire. The cattle has got a whiff of the smoke, an' they're bunching up."

Without further questioning, or seeing fit to answer, Amos spurred his horse on up the trail. The man's story had established the fact that the forest fires had been set. The combine had boldly started to wipe out his cattle!

In the shelter of a fringe of timber to the left of the head of the trail Amos Brodick halted and considered the situation from every angle. The cattle were indeed bunching almost in the center of the big expanse of table-land. Around this plateau there was a sparse growth of timber leading to the ridges in the west and south and sloping down in the north and east. Already the smoke from the fire was beginning to drift across the plateau—and this drifting smoke gave Amos an idea.

"Where did the shots come from?" he asked the punchers, who had been in charge of the cattle. "Which direction, I mean?"

"Seemed to me like they come mostly from the north side, an' maybe a few from the east," replied one of the men, pointing across the plateau.

"Martin an' his gang are hidin' in the timber," said Amos. "I'm goin' to drive 'em out along with the cattle! Here, string out, you fellows—in the timber down the west side there. Shoot on sight if you meet anybody. When you get below the line from west to east where the cattle are bunching up, put a match to the timber. It'll burn faster'n lightnin' in this wind, an' it'll shoot a powerful lot of smoke across that north end of the plateau. When the smoke starts we'll ride out an' get the cattle started this way."

"But the grass on the plateau?" exclaimed Williams.

"It's pretty well eaten down," said Amos; "it won't burn any too fast. It's the smoke from the timber I want. Hurry up, men—get goin'!"

When the smoke from the newly set fires began to roll out across the table-land, augmented by more smoke from the fires in the valley below the south ridge, Amos and the other dashed out upon the plateau and, firing their guns in the air, began to drive the cattle at a furious pace toward the south trail. Choking and gasping in the smoke they virtually stampeded the herd in the direction of the trail.

A scattering volley of shots came from the north side of the plateau, which now was submerged in a pall of smoke, riding eastward on the wind. The shots soon ceased, and Amos and Williams galloped ahead to guide the cattle into the head of the trail. The first flaming forerunners of the forest fire below were licking at the fringe of timber just to the west of the head of the trail when the cattle passed thundering down toward the valley.

Amos Brodick plunged on, ahead of the herd. Smoke and sparks filled the air as the fire raced eastward down the slopes of the valley. The rapidity with which the fire gained ferocious headway was astounding but not unnatural, for the timber, under-brush, and grass had known no rain in weeks of drought, and the forest and floor of the valley were sear and dry. Fanned by the wind, which increased in velocity as the clouds above Telltale Peak thickened in certain harbinger of a storm, the flames literally tore on their way, leaping from treetop to treetop, enveloping the trunks of trees in a fiery sheet, racing through the underbrush and along the ground.

On both sides of the valley the fire was raging and eating down toward the creek-bed and toward the trail, over which hung a thick curtain of smoke pierced by sparks and flying embers—a hot, suffocating blanket that shut out the rays of the sun and bathed the floor of the narrow valley in a weird, unnatural, saffron-colored light, which distorted the perspective and even hid the flames so dangerously near.

When the cattle reached the bottom of the trail they were between two walls of fire with the smoke-pall closing down upon them. There was fire behind them also, for the flames had swept from side to side in the head of the valley. In a rift of the dense, suffocating curtain above and ahead, Amos caught a glimpse of men topping a ridge far down the creek. Then the wind closed the gap and shut off his view.

"Stampede 'em down the trail," he shouted above the sullen roar of the burning forest. "Martin an' his men are goin' to try to head us off down the creek!"

The men galloped back and forth behind the plunging herd, firing their guns and shouting madly, while Amos Brodick rode far ahead of the cattle, his eyes fixed in a stare as he strove to pierce the curtain of smoke.

Some miles below, the valley would widen out; cliffs of limestone and ledges and rim-rock strewn with boulders and shale would impede the progress of the fire. If the cattle could be driven below this point, where the sides of the valley would close in for a short distance, they would be safe from the flames. The men, too, would have to pass this point to reach safety.

If the place was blocked by enemies it might mean death for both cattle and men. Amos Brodick's gun was in his hand as he galloped down the trail. Surely the men left at the ranch would be riding up the valley, for the smoke of the fire must long since have been seen by them.

Now a new factor added to the uncertainty. It became noticeably darker under the pall of smoke. The storm was gathering in the west, drawing a thick veil of clouds over the sunset. Night would come speedily. To get the cattle through in the darkness would be a herculean task.

A gust of wind broke the smoke curtain ahead, and, as Amos Brodick took advantage of the fleeting view, his pulses throbbed with uncertainty and apprehension. There were mounted men in the bottleneck of the valley ahead.

# CHAPTER XXIV
## INFORMATION

STANDING motionless on the edge of the limestone which capped a rise of ground below the east slope of Angel Butte, Neil watched the lone rider coming toward him at a furious pace on a big, powerfully built black horse. He recognized the magnificent steed which the man rode before he could make out with certainty the identity of the rider in the saddle. When he saw that the man approaching him was Left Hand he became aware of the fact that he too had been recognized.

Left Hand was gesturing toward him with his hat.

Neil quickly repressed an instinctive desire for flight when he recollected that his own mount could not be expected to outrun Left Hand's horse, and that, since the man was an outlaw himself according to reports, he had nothing to fear from him. He remembered, too, that he had caught sight of Left Hand standing in the front doorway of the Prairie Flower when he made his hurried exit by the rear.

He climbed down from the top of the rise, mounted, and rode boldly out into the open as Left Hand came pounding up with a serious expression on his face.

"You didn't go on over the butte, then!" exclaimed the gunman. "Lentu would have stopped you if you had, I guess. What're you doing—hidin' out down here?"

"I was waiting to see what would happen," confessed Neil.

"You needn't worry," said Left Hand curtly. "I told 'em I cracked Ratty from the doorway. Lentu beat it fast; but I guess the bartender sort of believed me. He knew Ratty had identified me an' probably thought I had it in for him for that reason. Anyway, it'll bother 'em if they figure on startin' anything."

"You—you mean you—took—the—blame!" stammered Neil.

"Oh, I didn't do what I did because of any sympathy for you, nor for friendship's sake, either," said Left Hand. "I had my reasons, an' I haven't got the time to explain 'em now. You goin' to the ranch?"

"Do you think it's—er—safe?" asked Neil anxiously.

Left Hand's contempt shone in his eyes. "You're a sorry sight. Look here, Sterret, it's time you woke up to a few things. You've been actin' like a fool. The West isn't a case of chaps an' handkerchiefs aroun' the neck an' guns that go off permiscuously. It's a case of men playin' the part of men whether for good or bad—you've got to go all the way one way or the other. Don't you see your uncle's got a whole lot of trouble on his hands? It's life or death with him. There's a bunch of mean-thinking, hard-shooting hombres in the game against him. Just for my own information I'd like to know what side you're on!"

"Uncle Amos never told me he was in such a peck

of trouble," said Neil surlily, his anger again swiftly rising against this man.

"It isn't one of those things you can talk much about—to a kid that's got a lot of fool notions in his head," retorted Left Hand. "You've got a pair of eyes an' some ears, haven't you? You can see an' hear, can't you? Don't you know Lentu's been fillin' you with a lot of soft stuff—catering to you with good reason? Why? Because Lentu and that outfit is figurin' to get your uncle an' get him cold. They know you're due to inherit the ranch, an' then they think they'll twist you round their little finger an' make you dance to their tune—an' maybe make you the goat in the end for the whole business. Oh, you're smart, all right. Why, for all I know you may be in on the deal; maybe you want the ranch so bad—"

"That's a lie!" cried Neil hotly. "That's a lie, Left Hand, an' you know it!"

"I hope so," said the other with a sparkle in his eyes. "But it looks a little that way. Maybe you've just been slow to see how things stood. Maybe they've had you buffaloed."

"Wait a minute, Left Hand!" cried Neil. "While you're doing so much talking maybe you'll tell me who you are."

"I'm Left-hand Smith," was the smiling reply.

"That gives a lot of information," Neil said with a sneer. "Where did you come from when you got back to the butte that night after Swain was killed? Tell me that!"

Left Hand eyed him curiously. "I came from the Smith River country."

"Sure; and it was over that way that Swain was killed."

"Do you know who killed Swain?" Left Hand asked quickly.

Neil avoided the eyes which stared at him. "Maybe that's why I was asking where you had been on that ride," he said boldly.

"No, it wasn't. But I'll tell you what I was over there for. I went over to see the forest ranger. Now come on, we'll hit for the ranch by a trail I know on the east side of the butte. I overheard 'em planning something up at the Double S last night, an' maybe there's trouble in the air. You can come along or stay—it's up to you."

Neil watched the man swing his horse up toward the slope. After a moment of indecision he followed. Up and up they rode on a dim trail, which led through the sparse timber growth, until they reached the top of the last slope under the crest of the butte. Here Left Hand paused and pointed toward the north. Neil looked and cried aloud in his amazement. The entire north slope was wreathed in smoke, and a line of fire was racing eastward toward the homestead shacks on the plain and the town of Angel. Already the north of twenty-two, where Left Hand's shack had stood, was a blackened vista instead of waving tufts of grass. The fire was sweeping eastward on the high wind at a fearful rate.

"That's some of your friend Lentu's work," Left

Hand called back. "Done to keep the folks down to Angel busy while they do their dirty work up here, an' to discourage the homesteaders."

He swung his horse into the trail which wound around the east side of the summit of the butte and down toward the ranch. When they came out of the timber on the south side Left Hand pointed again, up the valley this time, as he urged his horse to as great a speed as the trail would allow.

As Neil looked up the Wild Horse Valley he saw the smoke signal rising from the right spur of Telltale Peak. More than that, he saw other veils of smoke, lower down, drifting up from the timbered slopes at the head of the valley.

They arrived at the ranch within a few minutes. The men were throwing saddles on their horses in the corral. Mrs. French and Dora were out in the yard looking up the valley.

"Where is Uncle Amos?" Neil shouted to Dora as he drew rein with Left Hand at the main gate.

Dora came running toward him with an anxious face. "He's up the valley," she answered. "Oh, Neil, he saw the signal and went up there with Williams and some of the other men. He said there must be trouble with the cattle on the plateau range. And now, Neil, the men say there's a forest fire up there."

Left Hand had ridden through the gate directly to the corral. Neil saw him talking to the men; it looked as if he was giving orders. Mrs. French came running toward Neil.

"Your uncle said you and two of the men were to stay at the ranch if the others went up the valley," she said.

"Have some one else stay in my place," Neil shouted as he turned his horse. "I'm goin' up there." He drove in the spurs and galloped up the road, passed the upper fields and pastures, and entered the broad trail which led straight up the creek.

Far ahead he could see a pall of smoke hanging over the upper valley. Even as he looked the outlines of Telltale Peak were lost in the haze and then blotted out by the dense, rolling banners of smoke. The clouds had gathered high in the west, and dusk was beginning to fall. The wind was stronger. Thunder muttered in the distant skies, and then Neil wondered if what he had heard might not be the echoes of shots reverberating among the hills.

He was conscious of a new feeling, a new sensation; something within him seemed to have changed. He was sober, serious, and yet he sensed an unusual exhilaration as if he were freed from something which had been gnawing at his spirit. He thought of Swain, shot from behind, and a new kind of anger thrilled him; he thought of the burning prairie, of the raging fire ahead, of his uncle charging into the very teeth of it all, and he was strangely glad—relieved.

Close behind him he heard the hammer of hoofs and turned to look as a horseman shot past him. It was Left Hand galloping like mad up the trail on his splendid black steed.

# CHAPTER XXV
## BEFORE THE FLAMES

A MOS Brodick did not check the speed of his galloping horse when he glimpsed the unknown
riders in the neck of the valley through which he and
his men and his cattle must pass to safety. He plunged
ahead under the deepening smoke curtain with one
thought outstanding in his mind; cattle and men
simply must get through the neck, and before dark.

He now was far ahead of the herd, although he could
hear the thunder of the flying hoofs above the roar of
the wind and fire and the increasing muttering of the
approaching storm. There was but scant possibility
that the storm would break in time to stop the ravage
of the flames and leave the upper part of the valley
safe. The cattleman realized, too, that there would be
no stopping of that wild, stampeding, frightened herd
of cattle until the terrorized animals had passed the
neck between the upper and lower valleys and had
spread out in the wide space below and recovered,
undriven and unharassed, from the nameless fear
which possessed them.

Now a second rift in the drifting smoke veil ahead
gave Amos another glimpse of the men in the neck of
the valley. There were several of them, one or two on
each side and three in the center of the gap. They had
dismounted and apparently were working at something, holding their nervous horses by the rein and

bending and twisting at their mysterious task. One man was mounted and evidently directing the activity of the others.

As the smoke closed downward again, shutting off his view, Amos quickly surmised the thing which the men ahead were doing. At this strategic point a barbed-wire fence had been stretched across the valley from the rockbound sides late the previous summer. This fence had been put there to prevent the cattle grazing in the lower valley from drifting to the upper section. It had been a necessary precaution. In the spring, when the beef cattle were driven up the valley to the early-summer range, the wire had been pushed back to the rock walls to leave the trail open. It would have been strung across the neck again when the herd was on the late-summer range down the valley.

The combine forces now were stretching the wire across the gap, tightening it and making it fast to a few scattered trees near the center of the pass. When the terrorized forerunners of the stampeding herd hit this wire it would tumble them over. The cattle, pushing on from behind, would pile up, and soon the entire herd would be a struggling mass, choking the gap, trampling, stamping, pounding, smothering, dying in the racing flames and stifling smoke of the fire, cutting off the escape of the men behind, and leaving no evidence against the men who had brought about the catastrophe.

It was a fiendish plan, and in his brief interval of mental reflection, Amos Brodick saw that this had been the program of his enemies from the start. The fires had purposely been set at the head of the valley; the two men in charge of the herd had been prevented from starting the cattle down, to give the flames ample opportunity to gain sufficient headway; little resistance had been offered when Amos and the others had arrived on the plateau.

Martin and his aids had deliberately and successfully driven them into a trap!

Amos had a sickening, maddening sense of running into the teeth of insurmountable odds as he spurred his horse unhesitatingly toward the gap, and toward the barrier which he knew his enemies were prepared to enforce with bullets. Having gone this far, it was a fight to the death. There was no doubt in Amos Brodick's mind as to who had been responsible for Swain's death. He had known the moment he heard it that it was the work of the combine—a warning to him. Neither was there any skeptical view to be taken of Martin's confessed animosity toward him. There had been truth in what Martin had said that morning of the celebration in Angel; Amos had avoided the other rancher since the Sand Creek affair; and though Martin had no reason to fear that Amos' lips would not remain sealed about the whole cowardly business, neither Martin nor Lentu had been sure of it; hence the effort to involve him in the range war against the encroaching homesteaders, and this new plan to ruin him and probably kill him and let the forest fire wipe out the evidences of the crime.

The smoke curtain thickened, and the hazy atmos-
phere below it became shot with sparks. A forked
tongue of lightning blazed above, followed by the first
deafening crash of thunder. Amos saw the horse,
ridden by the one man ahead who remained in the
saddle, veer suddenly and leap in his direction. The
rider, who had been leaning far to one side directing
the men working with the wire, was thrown out of the
saddle and dragged by one stirrup as the frightened
animal dashed up the valley in long bounds.

Amos' face turned nearly purple with rage when he
recognized the features of Martin bobbing as his
shoulders were rapped upon the ground. Then
Martin's gun spoke, and the horse stumbled to its
knees. Martin dropped his gun in his haste to clear
himself of the horse. Amos, white-faced now with
burning fury, leaped from his own mount to confront
his archenemy. He had lost all consciousness of the
situation in which he was placed; he thought only of
confronting Martin and punishing him for his perfidy.
Shoving his own weapon into its sheath, he flew at
Martin in a grim frenzy of rage, to deal out with his
hands the retribution which he knew was due the man.
His fingers closed on Martin's throat as the other recognized him with bulging eyes, terror-stricken.

Back and forth in the trail and on the gravel and
grass of the creek bank Amos and Martin fought.
Although evenly matched in the matter of weight and
strength and age, Amos had the advantage of a right-
eous cause and the added incentive of a fury which

made him a veritable demon of vengeance. Martin would prove no match for him in that terrible struggle. He realized this and, clutching at Amos Brodick's flying fists with one hand, drew a knife from his belt with the other.

A scream of unnatural laughter issued from Amos' lips as he knocked the knife aside as if it were a plaything and planted his left fist again in Martin's face. There was unspeakable fear in Martin's face now, for in the steady gleam of Amos Brodick's eyes he saw death for himself mirrored. Why didn't McCabe and the others come to his rescue? Even as he asked himself this despairing question he heard pistol shots from the gap and knew that help from that quarter now was improbable. There was fighting ahead in the pass.

Clouds of smoke rolled over and upon the struggling men. Glowing sparks and fiery embers showered down on them unnoticed. The hot breath of the burning timber was in the air about them. Their eyes smarted and watered. And above every other sound—the hiss and crackle of the fire, the thunder crashing in the skies, the wind howling through the gap—was the increasing roar of the stampeding herd plunging down the trail, coming closer and closer on its race for the pass, with men behind driving it remorselessly, while they choked and gasped in the smoke and flying, flaming debris of the fire.

Toward all this rode Left Hand and Neil and the others.

When Neil had nearly reached the gap between the

upper and lower valleys he took a short cut which led up a ridge, around which the creek and the trail circled to some distance southward. As he reached the top of the ridge a startling sight unfolded before him.

The head of the valley was entirely shrouded in a dense blanket of smoke in which tongues of fire leaped and played. Through the gap he could see now and then the forms of two men locked in what appeared to be a death struggle. In the neck of the pass Left Hand was charging into the smoke toward a group of riders near the center. Neil could see the red flashes from Left Hand's gun as he galloped into the gap. From the ridge to the right a second body of men was riding down. Neil soon recognized Lentu in the lead.

Behind all this were the billows of smoke, the darkened skies, flashes of fire and lightning, the crashing detonations of thunder, and a sullen roar coming nearer and nearer—cattle running wildly for the outlet to the lower valley!

Now Left Hand's horse darted off to one side, rearing and plunging as his rider reloaded his weapon. Puffs of smoke began to spring into the wind from Lentu and the other riders charging down from the north. In the brilliant light from a flash of the impending storm Neil saw clearly the unmistakable form of his uncle in the smoke and sparks that filled the upper valley just beyond the gap. Another figure was reeling back from a rain of blows. Martin! And Neil had once thought his uncle was afraid!

The youth's face and neck flushed with shame as he drew his gun and galloped madly down the ridge straight for the gap and the converging lines of horsemen. Bullets whistled past him, and he heard the welcome sound of the other men from the ranch pushing their horses at breakneck speed down the ridge behind him. A fusillade of shots greeted Lentu and the others as they reached the floor of the valley.

Then riderless horses dashed down the trail, and Neil and the men behind him rode straight for the gap through which Left Hand had passed.

As they neared the gap they could see Amos Brodick staggering toward them, dragging a dead weight. The sharp staccato of pistol shots came from within the gap. Two riderless horses dashed out. Then they discerned in a rift of the swirling smoke that Amos was striving to pull his senseless enemy to safety; for behind him appeared a bobbing line of black, coming on and on, kicking up clouds of dust that mingled with the heavy-hanging, rolling smoke; snorting, bellowing, staring with reddened eyes and mad with terror—the stampeding herd.

Neil and the others shouted shrilly in their efforts to warn Amos of his danger of being trampled to death—an end which seemed certain with the rapid onrush of the cattle. The cattleman, having vanquished his enemy, now was showing the stuff which made the spirit of the West a synonym for courage and fairness, by trying to save him.

Tears of pride and admiration and terror welled in

Neil's eyes, and his heart throbbed in his throat, leaving him gasping and speechless as he saw that it would be impossible to reach his uncle before the plunging, thundering herd. His hands dropped at his sides as his horse reared and half turned in the hot breath of the fire and smoke. He would have covered his eyes, but he hadn't the power to move a muscle. An inarticulate wail of anguish died on his tongue as he saw Left Hand riding like the wind toward Amos Brodick.

Half a minute—perhaps less—and the cattle would be upon the man afoot and his burden. Over Left Hand's head and left side a rope was whirling in a wide noose. Suddenly it shot through the smoke and spark-filled air. True as a bullet whistling toward its mark it flashed, dropped over Amos Brodick's shoulders, and tightened instantly as Left Hand eased it to its hold on the horn of his saddle. Then the magnificent black responded to its master's command and leaped. Amos Brodick was jerked from the ground, his hold upon Martin's collar was pulled free, and in another few seconds he was dragged to the shelter of a mass of rock close to the right wall within the gap.

Out of the pass several men rode, holding their hands high above their heads, their horses plunging and snorting. Neil and the others with him covered them with their weapons and drove them back against the south wall on the outside of the gap. From the black and smoke-streaked sky overhead came a series of vivid flashes of lightning, and Neil, whirling his horse to look within the gap, saw the figure of Martin lying motionless in the path of the cattle, almost under the flying hoofs.

The heavens shook with the crashing, ear-splitting artillery of the storm, and then opened to let down the rain in blinding torrents upon the burning forest. The men huddled at the sides of the gap as the thundering herd swept through the pass, shaking the earth and walls of rock until the very air seemed to tremble with the smashing, grinding, pounding impact of hoofs.

With the rain the heavens grew lighter, and, when the cattle had passed, Neil looked wonderingly about him. Williams and the men who had been driving the cattle before the fire had halted before the little group of horsemen and were staring darkly at the prisoners. There was no sign of Lentu, but three forms could be distinguished upon the north slope; one of them was crawling down, while two were motionless, huddled in grotesque postures against the brown earth and rock down which coursed rivulets of water.

Neil turned his horse into the gap. He saw Left Hand's black horse standing in the lee of the rocks where he had dragged Amos Brodick out of the path of the herd. Left Hand was upon the ground, bending over a motionless form. But was it motionless? Neil saw his uncle raise an arm. He was alive. Left Hand had taken the one possible, desperate chance to save Amos Brodick's life and it had succeeded.

With a cry of joy Neil spurred his horse toward the figures in the shadow of the rocks.

# CHAPTER XXVI
## A NUMBER OF ARRESTS

AMOS Brodick's face lit with a rare smile as Neil knelt beside him and gripped both his hands in a warm, tight clasp. Unable to speak because of his joy that his uncle was alive, his feeling of shame that he could have suspected that his uncle had been cowed by the combine, Neil remained silent, retaining his grip of Amos Brodick's hands and smiling bravely into his eyes. Left Hand remained aloof, himself smiling whimsically and regarding the youth with new interest.

"There, there, Neil, don't try to squeeze my fingers off," said Amos with an attempt at gruffness. "We've had a little trouble, but it looks like it was over. You better put your slicker on, for it's rainin' like speckled wild cats."

"Are you all right, uncle; are you sure you're all right?" asked Neil brokenly and anxiously.

"I'm fine and fit," averred Amos stoutly, although he groaned as he slowly sat up under the leaning rock. "Just a bump or two that I was fool enough not to miss on the way over here. By Jiminy, Smith, you just naturally roped an' threw an' dragged me like I was a bull calf on the way to a brandin'!"

Left Hand laughed softly. "It was rough work, all right, Brodick—dog-goned rough work, I'll allow. But it was the only way I could see to get you out from in front of that herd in time. If you stayed there a few seconds longer you'd been trampled to death certain for sure, an' I took a chance on jerkin' you over here, thinkin' a broken arm or leg or sprained back wouldn't be as bad as gettin' run over by a bunch of stampedin' steers, an' that if it broke your neck, well—that would have been quicker an' easier than the other, maybe."

"Man, man, I ain't blamin' you none," said Amos with a good-natured scowl. "You saved my life, Smith. I hear they call you Left Hand on account you can draw an' shoot so swift on that side, but I say you can throw a mighty slick rope with that left of yours into the bargain. An' how about—what became of—"

"Martin?" asked Left Hand in a low voice that seemed cheerful. There was a satisfied gleam in his eyes as he shot a glance out into the downpour toward a dark spot which showed against the pools of water in the tracks left by the cattle.

"Yes. What of him?" Amos Brodick seemed to anticipate the answer.

Left Hand slowly shook his head. "He didn't get away."

"The cattle went over him?" said Amos with a shudder.

"The whole herd," replied Left Hand. "All they left was a shadow. And just what he deserved!" he added grimly.

Williams, the acting foreman of the 3-X-Z, Brodick's outfit, came riding up to them. "We took the guns away from that bunch out there," he told Amos.

"Got 'em herded under guard. McCabe an' Pierson are in the bunch."

Left Hand tossed his head angrily. "Lentu?" he asked sharply.

"Made his get-away when he saw how things was lookin' in the gap, the boys who came up with Neil say. Left two of his men dead an' one badly hit—Ben, the Double S cow-puncher. He's cussin' Lentu right an' left for bein' a quitter an' a dirty double-crosser an' gettin' him plugged."

It was now nearly dark with the rain continuing to fall in a steady deluge. Although the air was still thick with smoke and steam, it was cooler.

"I'll want to talk to Ben," said Left Hand, while Williams stared with a puzzled expression first at Amos Brodick and then at Left Hand.

Amos nodded toward the gunman. "Smith's in charge, now, Williams."

"We'll have to get you out of here first," said Left Hand, looking at Amos. "I expect you're too sore to ride to—"

"There's a cabin and some corrals 'bout a quarter of a mile below here on the south side of the creek," Amos interrupted. "I can make it that far with a couple of men to steady me, an' after a rest I'll be all right."

Left Hand gave his orders quickly. "Send a man back here, Williams, to help Neil get his uncle down to that cabin. Somebody will have to lead their horses. Brodick's horse has bolted. But don't pay any attention now to the horses that are gone, or the cattle. They can be rounded up an' seen to in the morning. I'll take a look out here where Martin was run over, an' then we'll take the prisoners down to the cabin, too—keep 'em there tonight. There's plenty to do tomorrow. That's right," he concluded as he saw Neil take the slicker from his saddle and offer it to his uncle.

"Put it on, Brodick; don't be squeamish. And, Williams, send a man who's got a fast horse down to the ranch for some bandages an' coffee an' sandwiches, an' some whisky—if they've got it—an' tell him to ride like blazes!"

As Williams left to carry out the orders Left Hand mounted the black and rode quickly out into the upper valley. He returned as Neil and Walt Frost were helping Amos Brodick out of the gap.

Amos looked at him inquiringly.

"Martin an' two others were killed by the cattle," said Left Hand briskly. "The other two might have been shot before," he added cheerfully, "but the cattle finished the job."

He saw that Amos was progressing all right, aided by Neil and Frost, and then went to join the men with the prisoners.

Night had descended as the injured men and the cavalcade of riders reached the cabin and corrals. There were two rooms in the cabin, and in one of these McCabc, Pierson, and the other men captured, were quartered with two armed guards sitting in the doorway watching them. The cabin had been used by men looking after the cattle in the valley; it contained

197

a stove, some rude furniture, a cupboard filled with dishes, and some foodstuffs, a lamp, and a lantern. The lantern was swung from the roof of the room containing the prisoners, and the lamp placed on a table in the other room which contained also four bunks, two superposed on each side of the room, and a stove at one end.

The wounded cow-puncher was placed upon one of the lower bunks, and Amos Brodick rested in the other. Williams built a fire in the stove after ordering the horses unsaddled and put into the corral. The saddles were piled in a corner of the room occupied by the 3-X-Z men, Left Hand, and the wounded Ben.

Left Hand examined the Double S puncher and found him mortally wounded in the left side. The man was delirious by spells, and groaned and swore fearfully in his lucid intervals, asking for water, which Left Hand gave him.

"You're going out, man," said Left Hand in a kind voice. "I'm afraid you haven't a chance with that hole in your side. Where did you fellers come from, Ben?"

"It's Lentu's work," cried Ben in a mixture of rage and pain. "He's a dirty quitter. Said they wouldn't have a chance to hang anything on us; wouldn't be anything left to tell who done it when the fire an' cattle got through wiping out the traces. An' he turned an' run at the first sign that things was goin' wrong; first—breeze of—bullets drove—him—off."

"That's Lentu's style every time," said Left Hand, laving the dying man's brow with cool water. "He's never been known to give a thought for anybody but himself. He doesn't care how many are killed in his schemes if he makes his get-away with a whole hide. You oughta have known him, Ben. Tell me, who set the fires, Ben?"

As the puncher tried to rise to a sitting posture, Left Hand addressed Amos Brodick, Neil, and the others aside. "Listen to this—if he talks," he warned them. "Who set the fires, Ben? You don't owe this crowd you've been running with anything."

"Martin an' McCabe's men set 'em in the head of the valley," said Ben with an effort. "Lentu had us set the prairie blazing on the north slope o' the butte. Said it would teach the homesteaders a lesson an' keep 'em busy down at Angel while we fixed things—up—here. Lentu's scheme, an'—Martin's—an' McCabe's—"

"Shut up, you yellow rat!" roared a voice from the other room where the prisoners were. "What good is it going to do you to talk? You're the quitter, you yellow rat!"

In a bound Left Hand reached the doorway into the other room, and, hitting out between the guards who had been too startled to move, he knocked McCabe to the floor with a crashing blow to the jaw.

"I suppose you'll talk, eh?" said Left Hand in a voice trembling with anger. "You'll talk all right; but it'll be in a courtroom with a government charge over your head. Here, some of you gag him," he called to the 3-X-Z men.

In a few minutes McCabe was bound and gagged on

the floor against the far end of the second room. "If these fellows start anything shoot right into the bunch of them," Left Hand instructed the guards. "Let 'em have it for keeps. You've got the authority!"

He returned to his place beside the bunk whereon Ben was tossing weakly again in the throes of delirium. When the dying man next had a lucid interval he appeared too weak to speak. He swallowed a mouthful of the water Left Hand held to his lips and then swiftly sank into a stupor.

"I don't think there's a chance to hear anything more from him," said Left Hand turning to Amos Brodick. "He's lost too much blood to last much longer, an' he may never come out of it again—unless that feller gets here from the ranch with a bit of liquor in time. It might rouse him for a spell."

They sat quietly and watched the rapid breathing of the stricken man. There was no sound save the occasional crackling of the fire and the rain beating upon the roof of the cabin. Neil sat near his uncle and glanced continually at the stern face of the gunman who had dashed fearlessly into the gap toward the men of the combine and had so daringly saved his uncle from death under the hoofs of the stampeding cattle.

Suddenly Amos Brodick spoke. "They were stringing the wire when you came, eh, Smith? Was that what they was doing?"

Left Hand nodded. "The black went through it like it was a piece of binding twine," he said with a faint smile. "They'd have had the other strands up in a minute, though, an' piled up the cattle. I should have got up here this mornin', for I sneaked up to the Double S ranch house last night an' heard 'em planning this thing. But I follered Lentu down to Angel to see what he was up to down there." He looked quickly at Neil, and the young man remembered with a painful start the killing of Ratty.

But Left Hand shook his head warningly when Neil would have spoken.

A cry from the bunk where Ben was lying attracted their attention. The cow-puncher was staring with eyes of reason and vainly endeavoring to raise his head. Left Hand aided him and again offered him water. "What is it, Ben? Try to say it."

"They—wanted—to—get—Brodick," whispered Ben as a veil seemed to drop over his eyes and a red froth bubbled on his lips.

"Yes—yes?" cried Left Hand, while the others strained to catch any sound from the man's lips.

In another moment, however, Left Hand laid the head back upon the coat pillow he had arranged at the head of the bunk. "He's gone," he said softly. "Another mark checked up against Lentu. Lord! I can't think of that cur without—"

Neil drew back from the man in wonder as he saw his whole body become tense with the rage and hatred which burned in his flashing eyes. The gunman clenched his hands and compressed his lips into a thin white line as he stared, unseeing, over the heads of the others in the room. Only Amos Brodick, watching him in fascination, seemed unsurprised by the fearful intensity of the man's passion.

When the mood had passed Left Hand covered the face of the dead man. Hardly had he done this when the messenger who had been sent to the ranch returned, bringing coffee, whisky, sandwiches, cloth for bandages, and liniment.

Neil and Left Hand rubbed the liniment on Amos Brodick's bruises, while Williams made hot coffee.

"The cook sent word he'd bring the buckboard up at daylight for Amos," said the messenger.

"I think I'll be able to ride in the morning," returned Amos. "I'm good for a few years in the saddle yet, thanks to Smith, here. By golly, man, you sure didn't lose any time in thinking."

Left Hand merely smiled in answer, and then, as Williams was getting out the cups for the coffee, he stepped to the doorway into the other room and called to Pierson. The cattleman came to the doorway with a surly, questioning expression on his face.

"Come in an' have some coffee," Left Hand invited. "I'd like to have a little talk with you."

Pierson entered the room and sat down on a bench near the bunk where Amos Brodick was lying. "I'm not going to talk," he said. "You can save yourself the trouble, whoever you are, of asking me any questions." He looked at Left Hand, who laughed.

"Don't be a plumb fool, Pierson," said Left Hand. "We've got enough information from Ben besides what *I* know to put you fellers in the penitentiary, an' that's where you're all goin'—fast as you can be taken to The Falls an' given a fair trial. There's only one thing, Pierson, an' that's this: Some of you may not have to serve as much time as some of the others—say, McCabe, for instance. Have some sense."

Left Hand leaned toward the man and opened his shirt. All who were in the room started in surprise as they caught the gleam of a badge pinned to Left Hand's undergarment. He was standing, however, so that the prisoners in the other room could not see it through the doorway.

"I see," said Pierson, sneering in plain contempt. "I suppose they've promised you immunity from some of your own stunts to be an assistant ranger or a deputy of some kind. You're a rotter."

"That's a government badge, Pierson," said Left Hand softly. "McCabe an' you an' Lentu are up against the Federal game this time. There ain't goin' to be much leniency shown this trip."

Neil and the others had now recovered from their astonishment. Only Amos Brodick had the air of having known it all along. In an instant Neil realized why Left Hand had not drawn against Lentu the night of the celebration in Angel. He had wanted Lentu and the others to go ahead with their schemes and thus run into a government trap. He realized that the combine's move against the homesteaders and his uncle constituted a grave offense; but something in Left Hand's manner also convinced him that it was more than any promise such as Pierson had intimated, which had prompted the gunman's decision to accept the mission from the Federal authorities.

"Pierson, I have nothing against you," Left Hand was saying. "I took this job as a special inspector of the land office for different reasons than you think. You'll learn all this in time. I don't expect you to talk now. I'm just giving you a little friendly advice, for I believe you're the best of the crowd you've been herdin' with. I want you to think over what I'm telling you. Your crowd is going over for a good stiff term in the pen. Some of them may hang. McCabe an' Martin an' Lentu had their reasons for wanting to get Brodick mixed up in a deal where they'd have a club over his head. They used you for one of their tools, just like they used all the men with 'em on their ranches—just like they used that poor dead Ben, there. Now some of these men are goin' to talk before they get through with it. They're goin' to spill the whole thing from beginnin' to end—all they know. It'll make the court feel a little inclined in their favor, maybe. You don't owe as much as you think to McCabe an' the others. Just ponder this over between here an' the jail in The Falls, an' see if it wouldn't be showin' good sense on your part to get yourself off with a light sentence. This is just friendly advice from me an' I ain't goin' to say no more about it."

Left Hand rose and, after drinking a cup of coffee, got his saddle from the pile in the corner.

"It's gettin' on toward morning," he said to Amos,

"an' I've got to hit Lentu's trail. Take McCabe, Pierson, an' their crowd down to the ranch in the mornin' an' send word to the deputy in Angel. He'll come after 'em to take 'em to The Falls. Likely the forest ranger an' his guard from Telltale will be along asking about the fire, an' they'll help with the prisoners. You an' your men are special deputies now, an' that bunch in there an' Pierson here are under arrest. I'll likely be back this afternoon."

Neil followed him out of the door. The storm showed signs of beginning to let up. Rain still was falling, but in lessened volume, and the wind had abated.

"I suppose the deputy'll be wanting to take me along," he said to Left Hand.

"Never mind about that till the time comes," said Left Hand as he strode away in the darkness toward the corral to get his horse.

# CHAPTER XXVII
## ON ANGEL BUTTE

NEIL could not avoid thinking about his predicament as the morning approached. It was plain that Left Hand had assumed the responsibility for the killing of Ratty to shift the blame from Neil temporarily. What his object was in so doing Neil could not fathom. Neither could he tell his uncle about the matter in the presence of the others and after Left

Hand had admonished him to be silent. Although the mystery of Left Hand's identity and his purpose in that section of the country had apparently been explained, there were still several angles to the business which were as puzzling as ever.

At dawn the cook arrived from the ranch with the buckboard, and preparations were speedily made for the departure from the cabin. Amos Brodick rode in the buckboard in advance of the cavalcade of horsemen, McCabe, Pierson, and the others riding closely guarded by the 3-X-Z men. As Left Hand had predicted, the forest ranger and the guard from Telltale Peak arrived early on the scene and, after hearing an account of what had happened from Amos Brodick, joined the men escorting the prisoners.

There seemed scant possibility of Lentu and any he might have with him attempting to attack the men guarding the prisoners and release them on the way to the ranch. Nevertheless the party kept a sharp lookout going down the valley and was prepared to frustrate any such design. It had stopped raining, and the sun had come out bright and clear.

McCabe rode sullen and frowning, keeping his eyes upon the horn of his saddle, his hands tied behind his back, as were those of Pierson and the others. The men were mostly silent, but an occasional grumble led Neil to believe that Left Hand's prophecy that the men would be willing to talk would be fulfilled.

The cattle were discovered grazing far down the

valley, apparently none the worse for their experience of the day before.

Neil heard the forest runner telling Williams that Left Hand had visited him at his headquarters on Smith River, and that he had expected trouble. He said it was his belief that in securing the services of Left Hand as a special officer the government had carried out a plan to fight fire with fire in the matter of dealing with the combine.

"The government sent a man just as speedy with his gun as any they had on their side," said the ranger. "I had instructions to give him any assistance he might ask for, and that I could give, but he told me he could handle the situation alone. Well, I guess the 3-X-Z outfit helped, all right."

"But he ain't got Lentu yet," said Williams in a worried voice. "I'll bet Lentu's well on his way out of the country."

"Don't believe it," replied the ranger. "He'll try to get this Left Hand, mark my words."

When the guards and prisoners finally rounded the last bend in the wide trail above the upper pasture and came in sight of the ranch house they saw the buckboard standing at the main gate, while Amos Brodick was listening to Dora and Mrs. French. They appeared to be in great excitement, talking rapidly and gesturing up the creek and toward Angel Butte.

Neil and the forest ranger spurred their mounts ahead of the rest and soon arrived at the ranch house. They saw Amos disappearing within the house, followed by Mrs. French, who was still talking.

Dora came running toward Neil, her face showing pleasure and relief at finding him unhurt; it showed also that she was greatly excited and the bearer of news.

"Oh, Neil, I am glad you are safe," She exclaimed as he checked his horse and looked down upon her seriously.

"What are you and Mrs. French so excited about?" he asked. "Uncle is safe and the cattle got out. Why, Dora, are you crying?"

There were tears in the girl's eyes. "I'm so glad," she said again. "But, Neil, there have been more than a hundred men at the ranch this morning from Angel—the big posse, and every man is armed and Lentu is leading them!"

"Lentu!" cried Neil. "A posse? What—what are they after? Who—"

"They're after Left Hand, Neil. Lentu told them in Angel that Left Hand had set fire to the prairie over there to stop them from following him after he had shot somebody in town. And, Neil, the whole town came near being burned and would likely have burned if it hadn't been for the rain coming just when it did."

"But Lentu—why, we saw Lentu late yesterday afternoon up the valley, and when we started shooting he fled for his life," said Neil in wonder. "He—he must have gone straight to Angel!"

He could not help but marvel at the man's courage and persistence. Then he remembered that Lentu was not aware that Left Hand was a Federal officer. He probably thought he could capture him and get the posse excited enough to hang him before they could learn the truth. He did not listen to Dora's explanation that one of the posse had said Lentu met them as they were leaving Angel at dawn. What if Lentu should succeed? Would it not absolve Neil of all connection with the murder of Ratty? Would they not accept his statement that he had fired high to scare Ratty, and wouldn't Lentu himself tell them that? Evidently they did not now believe that Neil had killed the dealer, for if they thought that, they would not be looking for Left Hand alone.

"They have got the butte surrounded," he heard Dora saying. "Did—did Left Hand kill somebody down there, Neil? You came back with him, didn't you, yesterday? And uncle says he saved his life."

Neil started guiltily. He looked at Dora. "No he didn't kill anybody," he heard himself saying suddenly. "Listen! What was that?"

From the direction of the summit of the butte came the sharp echoes of a volley of shots.

"They've cornered him up there!" cried Neil. "Did you women tell Lentu and the posse we were coming down this morning?"

Dora nodded.

"And Lentu thought Left Hand would cut off up the butte to look for him, and he led the posse up there!" Neil decided.

Amos Brodick came limping out of the house just as

the men with the prisoners arrived. "Let me take your horse," he called to Williams, and when he had mounted he motioned to the forest ranger. "We've got to go up there," he called, pointing toward the butte.

Neil wheeled his horse and joined them as they rode out of the gate, through the north pasture, and up the trail leading to the summit of the butte. His face was grim, and a determined light shone in his eyes. He pushed his horse into the lead and held him to as stiff a pace as the steepness of the trail would permit.

They heard more shots as they climbed the butte, scattering shots, and as they neared the summit they heard shrill shouts and the sound of many horses. As Neil urged his mount up the last steep pitch in the trail to the summit he felt a wild exultation in his blood as his body thrilled to a strong emotion. What was more, he knew the source of that thrill; knew it came from a new and satisfying sense of loyalty toward his uncle.

Deep down in his heart Neil realized that he had been a fool; he acknowledged that he had been mistaken in his conception of the West, had been foolish in his desire to pose as a member of the rough, wild school of men who had taken the law into their own hands and attempted to rule by the speed of their gun play and the intimidation of others less skilled with their weapons. He took pride in the courage of his uncle, in Amos Brodick's inherent respect for a square deal. He was wrathful now when he thought of the manner of Swain's death, and there no longer was any suspicion in his mind but that it had been Lentu and the men with him who had been attempting to run off the cattle that day and thus cause trouble and loss for Amos Brodick.

At the top of the final pitch in the trail Neil found himself in a jam of other mounted men. Some were leaping out of their saddles and running afoot toward the north side of the crest of the butte. Neil got off his own horse and followed them.

On the north side of the summit a strange sight confronted his eyes. Left Hand, unarmed, was standing white-faced before a group of shouting, maddened men. But Neil could tell by the flashing of Left Hand's eyes that he was not white-faced with fear but with almost uncontrollable rage and fury.

"That's the man you want," he heard Lentu crying. "He shot Ratty when Brodick's kid nephew an' I was having a little fun with him, shooting over his head. He set the prairie fire to help make his get-away. I saw him! He's a gunman with a record as long as from here to Angel, an' Ratty was just another notch on his gun handle, an' if the whole town had burned up he'd have laughed."

Neil tore his way through the crowd. "That's a lie!" he shouted to the men behind Lentu as he crowded between Lentu and Left Hand. "If anybody shot Ratty I shot him myself, although I was trying to fire over his head to scare him. That's the truth. And it was Lentu himself who set the prairie fires to cover up an attempt to kill my uncle and steal his cattle and to scare the homesteaders. One of the men with him confessed to that before he died yesterday."

With a roar of rage Lentu swung on Neil, but the youth dodged the blow, and the men behind Lentu held him back. Neil saw his uncle and the forest ranger pushing their way to his side. He saw, too, with a start of astonishment, that Dora had followed them and was on the summit of the butte.

"And that isn't all," Neil shouted to the mob of men crowding before him. "That man Lentu shot and killed my uncle's foreman, Swain, and I saw him do it. He told me to keep still and threatened to kill me if I told the truth!" Neil was looking at his uncle now.

"He lies!" screamed Lentu in a fury. The silence which had fallen over the men was shattered by a shot. Neil felt a blow high on his right side and was swung partly around with it.

He saw Lentu struggling with some men. Neil drew his gun and handed it to Left Hand behind him. "He'll try to get you," he said as he sagged to his knees.

Neil knew he had been shot. His uncle and Dora were soon supporting him. He saw Lentu break loose from the men and run to the edge of the rock on a corner of the summit and leap off.

The forest ranger held up his hands and began to speak. "This man is a government agent," he explained, "sent here to prevent Lentu and Martin and McCabe and the others with them from intimidating the homesteaders. Martin was killed with some others yesterday when they fired the forest up Wild Horse Creek and tried to kill Brodick's cattle and himself.

One of the men who died confessed that the prairie fire was started by Lentu. As for this shooting you are talking about, I know nothing concerning it."

Left Hand spoke now for the first time.

"You can blame Lentu for that into the bargain. I saw that play in Angel. If you had listened to me instead of to Lentu you would have learned something. Lentu got Sterret here to fire a couple of shots over Ratty's head to scare him, for Ratty was talkin' kind of mean about Sterret. The shots Sterret fired went over Ratty's head, an' you'll find 'em high in the wall. But with Sterret's second shot Lentu fired himself an' killed Ratty, likely so he could scare Sterret an' get him in his power in the deal against his uncle. Lentu had good reason, an' he has no more respect for a man's life than I have for a pack rat."

"We'll hang him!" shouted several of the men in the posse.

"No!" thundered Left Hand. "Absolutely not! I'll look after him." He opened his shirt to reveal the badge pinned beneath. "I want him on several counts—myself, understand. You are not to touch him."

He repeated this when the men continued to grumble, and finally they agreed to allow him to settle with Lentu. One of the men returned the gun which Left Hand had dropped when he had fallen in climbing to the summit of the butte. Lentu would doubtless have killed him when he was thus unarmed except for the presence of the posse.

Neil could see Left Hand striding across the summit of the butte and heard him as if from far away ask about his horse. Then Left Hand disappeared, and the others who were grouped around seemed to assume hazy shapes hard to distinguish. There was a low hum of voices in his ears. Hands were feeling at his side; tender hands which he knew were Dora's. He thought he heard his uncle swearing, but he wasn't sure. He felt as if he wanted to doze and closed his eyes. A numbness stole over him, and then everything was blotted out in black oblivion.

# CHAPTER XXVIII
## OUT OF THE TWILIGHT

GRADUALLY there came to Neil's ears a sound as of waves washing against a rocky shore. It grew fainter, then clearer, with a sort of musical rhythm that swelled until it resembled the clinking of cymbals at a distance, and when Neil opened his eyes at last he recognized it for the clattering of harnesses and the crunch of wheels against a road.

He saw the blue, sun-filled sky overhead and then became aware of Dora's face looking down upon him. He was aware, too, that she was holding his hands. A dull, aching pain throbbed in his side, as if in accompaniment to the click of shod hoofs and iron tires. He knew he was being transported in a spring wagon, but a question must have shown in his eyes,

214

for Dora spoke to him quickly.

"We are taking you to Angel where the doctor can look after you," she said in a sweet voice. "You mustn't try to talk or move, Neil; just keep quiet, and you will be all right."

He wondered vaguely at the sob in her voice. He remembered he had been shot. There was the pain in his side to remind him of that. But just how he came to be shot was a confused blur in his mind, the same as the sight of Dora's face now was blurred, and the sky seemed farther and farther away and becoming darker. He tried to grasp one of the girl's hands, but again the oblivion of senseless blackness intervened as he lost consciousness for the second time.

Then it seemed to Neil that there were innumerable intervals when he saw light and felt the throbbing pain in his side—a pain which also seemed to be in his head, his arms, and his neck—all through his body. He sometimes felt the burning sensation of a high fever, and he dreamed strange dreams and awakened suddenly many times to find himself talking. Water—water! Could he ever get enough water!

There was singing sometimes now, too; singing and shouts and shots. Then the hot breath of a forest fire would play upon his face; thousands upon thousands of steers would thunder by with a horrible racket, and he would just have time to leap clear of the flying hoofs and would awaken to find himself panting for breath.

In brief, lucid intervals he recognized Dora, dressed

in white, sitting near him. He was in bed, now; it was a white bed, and there were white window curtains fluttering on one side of the room. And he was thirsty—oh, so thirsty!

Once he recognized his uncle at his bedside, and with him was another man with a beard and spectacles, who held his wrist and watched him, his gaze burning into his own. The pain was not so bad now, but there was the sensation of the fever and the delirium which accompanied it; Neil tossed and turned in an agony of unrest, while his tortured mind made him the helpless prey of a thousand hallucinations and dreams in which there almost always figured two men—a burly, red-faced, evil-looking man, and another who was slender and dark and who smiled a cold, deadly smile.

At times when he dimly made out the figure of Dora beside him he imagined he saw tears in her eyes. Twice he tried to talk to her, but the words would not come. He had grasped her hand in a weak clasp once and felt the touch of her lips on his brow, but then had come again the delirium and the fever and the horrible, unquenchable thirst and aching of his hot fever-racked body.

Thus for three weeks Neil hovered between life and death, and just when it seemed that he must have entered the twilight preceding the long, long night of the grave, when the doctor whom Amos Brodick had brought from The Falls stayed two days and two nights at his bedside, he fell into a natural sleep which lasted most of the day and all of a night, and then he woke, with a moist brow and clear of eye, free of the fever and the delirium and the thirst.

He saw Dora and his uncle and the man whom he took to be the doctor. The latter smiled at him cheerfully, but immediately put his fingers across his lips to signify that he shouldn't try to talk.

"Young fellow, you can thank your stars for a good constitution," he said in an agreeable, gruff voice. "Now you must be still and quiet, and we'll give you a little nourishment; then you must sleep some more, and soon you'll be well."

Neil could see the bright sun shining outside the window, through which came a vagrant, sweet-scented breeze. Dora was busying herself arranging the pillows about him and smoothing the bed coverings. She smiled at him, and his uncle, too, appeared greatly pleased.

"They run in the family, doctor—those constitutions like Neil's," he said in a hearty voice. "He'll be all right now when he gets a few good feeds of beef an' mutton an' the like."

Neil smiled wanly, realizing that this pleasantry on his uncle's part was due to the elder man's joy in his recovery. It was good to know that people were glad one was going to get well. Neil sipped the orange juice and white of an egg Dora brought him, keeping his eyes on her face the while. When he once made as if to speak she placed a cool finger on his lips and shook her head.

"You must sleep again, Neil," she said sweetly.

And for another week that was what Neil did most of the time—sleep. His wound was dressed every day by the Angel doctor, and Neil was told it was healing rapidly.

"The doctor from The Falls took the bullet out, and you never knew it, did you?" Dora asked one morning after he had begun to talk again.

He shook his head. "But I felt a lot of pain in my right side," he said, smiling.

After a period of silence he asked about affairs at the ranch and learned that the regular work was progressing. The men who had been captured in the upper valley the day of the forest fire had been taken to the jail in Great Falls. His uncle had gone back to the ranch, but came down to see him every other day. A relative of Martin's had arrived from the East and had assumed charge of the Double S. Ben had been buried there, as had also Martin. Dora said she understood that Pierson had made a full confession to the authorities. The homesteaders were rebuilding their shacks, Left Hand had relinquished his claim, and two others had filed on the two quarters in the north half of section twenty-two. It appeared that Left Hand had merely filed on the land to draw the fire of the combine.

His uncle told him he had suspected the combine of doing away with Swain from the first, but that no effort to fasten the crime on any one had been made at the time, so the combine could be led into the trap of their own making, which had resulted in the death of Martin and five others and the capture of the rest, except—

"And Lentu?" Neil asked quickly.

"Lentu is hiding in the mountains," replied his uncle.

"Where is Left Hand?"

"Left Hand has been on his trail for a month but hasn't been able to catch up with him yet. But Lentu can't get away; the officers all over the State are on the lookout for him, and when he shoves his nose out of the hills he'll be captured—or killed. Left Hand is waiting for him, and he's liable to hit for Angel."

"You mean Lentu? Wouldn't he be foolish to do that?"

"Neil, my boy, Lentu is one of those men who can't forget that another has beaten him. He'll try to get even any way he can. He knows that sooner or later he must meet Smith—which is Left Hand's right name. An' Smith is not chasin' him so much as he's waitin' for him to come out—and fight."

"I should have known all along that Left Hand wasn't a hired gunman," Neil complained. "I even thought once, Uncle Amos, that maybe—that maybe what the combine said was true, and that you—that you had hired him for—for protection!" Neil blushed with shame as he finished his contrite statement.

But Amos Brodick merely laughed heartily. "I knew what Smith was here for, but he'd swore me to secrecy. It did look sort of bad for me—us—there for a while. An' I've never been much of a hand to confide in people; I should have told Swain and you and the rest more than I did."

"Uncle, how did Swain come to shoot the light out that night of the celebration when Left Hand and Lentu met?"

"Well, I think that was agreed upon by Left Hand and Swain," replied Amos. "You see, Left Hand had to meet Lentu to show him he wasn't afraid of him. That play on the horse in the afternoon and the play in the saloon that night was to sort of egg him on—to make the combine begin hostilities. Smith couldn't go up there an' arrest that bunch till he had a good respectable lot of evidence. An' he didn't want to kill Lentu that night, or it might lead to the establishment of his identity as an officer and scare the combine out. An' he wanted, too, I reckon, to see if Lentu knew him."

"Why, had they met before?" asked Neil, surprised.

"I reckon they did, some time."

"Did they have trouble, uncle? It seems as though Lentu would have recognized Left Hand without Ratty having to identify him."

"I guess maybe Lentu had forgotten him," said Amos with a reminiscent smile. "But he's likely to remember him the next time they meet. Now, Neil I've got to be going; Dora will stay down here in the hotel with you until you're well enough to come back on the ranch. The hunting season has started, an' I brought you down a couple of blue grouse today. Mrs.

French an' all the boys send their choicest regards, an' I'm afraid they'll try to make a hero of you when you get back for calling Lentu that a way in front of his gun an' gettin' shot up for doing it. Boy, I was right proud of you that day—"

But Neil had turned his face away. "I'm a long ways from being any hero, uncle, but I'm willing to learn a few things from now on," he said earnestly.

"That's the spirit, son," said Amos as he patted him on the back with a smile of genuine pleasure. "An' now here's your nurse to chase me away an' bring you some of that grouse, I expect."

Neil found it hard to take his eyes off Dora when she was in the room, and often when she was reading to him she would look up to find his gaze fixed on her; then she would flush and turn disconcertedly back to her reading.

But not once as the days passed and he finally became able to sit up in a chair and then to walk a little, did he speak to her of their unusual situation and their pact. Into his mind had come a strange thought which worried him, because he felt the force of it more and more as the days went by.

Was he worthy of her?

The land now was aflame with the golden browns and vivid crimsons and saffrons of autumn, and the high slopes of Angel Butte were splashed with color. The air was crisp, cool, and invigorating. Neil felt the blood bounding in his renewed body. And then came the memorable day when he first went downstairs, leaning upon Dora's shoulders, and ate in the hotel dining room. Soon after this he went down for each meal, and his uncle announced that within a week he would be taken back to the ranch.

One warm, sunlit afternoon Dora joined him where he was sitting on the lower porch and tried to prevail upon him to go to his room. She appeared worried and excited, and at first refused to acknowledge this until he had asked her again and again about the cause for her agitation. The men about the place, too, appeared thoughtful; they were unusually keen and somewhat expectant.

Finally Dora told him.

"Lentu and Left Hand are in town," she whispered.

# CHAPTER XXIX
## THE RECKONING

THE news sent a thrill vibrating in every fiber of Neil's body as he contemplated its significance. The meeting, which his uncle had declared inevitable, was at hand. Lentu had come out of the hills. Whether driven out by Left Hand or by that inexorable law which decrees that men of Lentu's stamp must meet an avowed antagonist or be forever branded as a coward, mattered not. Lentu had proved he was not afraid.

From Dora, Neil ascertained that the report of the arrival of the two gunmen had been whispered about town all morning. He turned aside in a kindly manner her entreaties that he avoid any excitement—if there should be reason for excitement. He asked the hotel runner for additional details and learned that the men had ridden in from the west at dawn, Lentu arriving in advance of Left Hand.

Their horses had shown unmistakable signs of long, hard riding, the dust being caked on their flanks and seamed with the dried courses of rivulets of sweat. Lentu had eaten in the café near the Prairie Flower and had disappeared, but had not been seen to leave town. Left Hand had had breakfast in the hotel and had then gone to a room for a few hours of sleep. Neither had mentioned the other.

Neil wondered that every one appeared so calm and outwardly disinterested. Men collected on the hotel porch to comment on the weather, the time of the two daily trains, the price of sheep and cattle—anything at all save the topic which must have been on the tip of every tongue and yet remained unspoken. Neil saw the deputy sheriff, Mills, sauntering to the post office, chewing a toothpick, apparently unconcerned. Yet Lentu was wanted on several charges. He was wanted for the murder of Ratty, the dealer; for the killing of Swain; for the firing of the prairie, thus burning the property of many homesteaders and threatening the town of Angel itself; for his association with Martin, McCabe, and the others of the combine in their unlawful scheme. It was generally known he was in town, but no move was made to take him into custody.

Very plainly, by their attitude, the county authorities and the townspeople were showing that the affair was to be settled without interference at that time from them. Left Hand's demand, that Lentu be left to him, was respected.

Neil could not help but remember with a quickening of the pulse the passionate fire which shone in Left Hand's eyes when he had stood before Lentu unarmed on the summit of the butte. He recalled, too, how Left Hand had looked that night in the cabin in Wild Horse Valley when he had told the dying Ben what manner of man he considered Lentu to be. What would happen when these two met? Neil felt the conviction growing within him that there was something between these men aside from the breaking of laws; something more sinister, more terrible than the disregarding of a man-made law could possibly be.

The town seemed strangely quiet in the sunshine of early afternoon. All about it stretched the golden plains, with here and there a vivid spot of color from the turning leaves of cottonwood or willow growing in some better-watered coulee; colors that grouped and ran riot on the higher slopes of the butte in the west. The air was rich with that peculiar, dry, earthy tang which is distinctive of the prairie lands climbing to the eastern foothills of the Rockies. The occasional bark of a dog and the clang of metal from the blacksmith shop were the only sounds heard. Now and then some drifting cloud of dust upon the plain betokened the approach of a horseman or a team. Such a cloud of dust from the west brought Amos Brodick in the buck-board to take Neil and Dora back to the ranch.

When Amos had taken the team to the hotel barn to be watered and fed and rested against the trip to the ranch in the cool of the late afternoon and the twilight, he stopped to talk to Neil on the porch before going in to eat lunch.

"I expected it," said Amos when he heard the news from Neil. "Came down here to settle it. He showed up twice on Smith River, I heard, but they simply didn't offer to arrest him. He had to come."

Amos looked up and down the street, shook his head thoughtfully, and without further comment, went in to eat. Dora hurried upstairs to arrange her own and Neil's belongings for transportation in the buckboard on the ride home. She, too, felt the significance of the hour, but hoped that they would be able to get started for the ranch before anything could happen.

Neil, leaning back in his chair, saw that several men were lounging around the west end of the porch, and as he looked down the street he made out other groups in doorways and before the stores and saloons. Interest seemed to be centered in the street instead of inside the various buildings, and in the very studied, listless attitudes of the groups was an intangible sug-gestion of tense expectancy.

Usually at this time of day there were many home-steaders and ranchers setting out for their homes, having finished the business which brought them to town. But this afternoon there was no movement to leave on the part of those who had come in in the morning. There were many horses tied to the hitching rails before the stores, while their owners, riders, or drivers lingered along the street.

Neil suddenly noticed a change in the attitude of the men about the hotel porch. Their low hum of conversation was hushed. They were looking down the street. Neil looked too, and started in surprise. Again came the hum of conversation, but it was very plainly forced and meaningless, more for effect than for any real purposes of discussion or information.

Lentu was coming slowly up the street.

He walked well within the shade of the shelters built over the fronts of some of the stores, and kept close to the buildings. He hardly glanced within the doorways he passed, as if by some subtle intuition he divined that no one whom he wished to see was within. Occasionally he replied to a guarded greeting or nodded to some one in the groups about the street.

As he came nearer Neil saw that this day Lentu wore two guns. He had removed his chaps, and the sheaths which held his weapons were strapped tight against his thighs. His big hat was pulled well down to shade his eyes; his black leather cuffs, worn smooth, gleamed with silver trappings. And ever his keen, searching, menacing gaze roved about the street from group to group, meeting the looks of others without a sign of flinching; audacious, bold, at times sneering, but ever alert.

When Lentu was across the street from the hotel he

halted for a look over the open square in the direction of the railroad station. Then he swung on his heel and walked quickly toward the hotel.

In the excitement which he had experienced in seeing the gunman, and in his anticipation of the meeting between him and Left Hand, Neil had actually forgotten that this was the man who had shot him, whom he had openly accused of killing Swain and thus defied. However he felt no particular anger toward the man, and it was not until Lentu actually put foot on the porch and flashed his gaze over Neil along with the others that he recollected he might possibly expect more violence.

He rose quickly to his feet with the instinct of self-preservation, but Lentu paid no further attention to him. Instead his eyes were turned toward the doorway leading into the hotel's small lobby. He stepped across the porch and seemed to slouch in a half crouch as he cautiously entered. He looked about the lobby and into the dining room and then warily stepped to the refreshment counter.

Neil, looking into the lobby through the window from the porch, saw his uncle enter from the dining room. A strange silence had fallen over those on the porch and within the hotel. The jingle of Lentu's spurs had echoed loudly, and now the clink of glasses was heard clearly as the bartender set out a drink in response to what must have been a silent signal from Lentu.

Now another step was heard—a light, catlike step

from the dining room. There was a faint jangle of spurs, and Left Hand glided into the lobby and paused almost in front of the door leading into the bar. Neil saw his face freeze into grim but distorted lines; it was white, furious, and held a glare of almost maniacal rage and hate in the eyes which slowly narrowed and gleamed steel-blue.

A sigh seemed to waver in the room and out upon the porch, as there was a long intaking of many breaths; and when Left Hand spoke, his words came like the crack of a whiplash.

"Don't move, Lentu. I can see you in the mirror!"

In the pause which followed Neil sensed that the two gunmen were staring into each other's eyes through the medium of the mirror behind the bar. Men who were standing directly behind Left Hand slipped silently aside. Amos Brodick was watching breathlessly from a place near the desk. Neil kept to the window, his eyes upon Left Hand's face and the left arm and hand which hung tense and as motionless as if it were modeled in bronze, above the butt of the pistol in the black sheath at the man's left thigh.

Left Hand spoke again, his words coming clear with a hint of tremendous passion behind them as he kept his gaze riveted upon the image he saw in the mirror.

"Lentu, the law wants you. The government has given me the authority to arrest you. You are wanted for murder and for leading a conspiracy against settlers on government lands. If you give up and allow yourself to be taken to The Falls you will be found guilty, and you'll hang like a rat till you're dead!"

There was a short, breath-taking interval of silence.

"Lentu, you can sneer at the gallows, for you'll never hang. You'll never hang, because you won't give up. I'd hate to see you give up! If I had thought there could be no hitch of justice and that you would hang I'd have arrested you before this or I'd arrest you now. But you might have a chance that way, and you can't have a chance, Lentu—not with me.

"I told you that the night we were alone in the shack on twenty-two; and now I'll tell you why. Think back, Lentu—think back a long time. Think back to that night up on Sand Creek—remember? Ah—you begin to remember, eh? The night you led the bunch that took two men out and murdered them—hanged them for a crime they were accused of but never tried for— hanged them after you had captured them under a white flag of truce!"

Neil glanced instinctively at his uncle, and for a brief instant Amos Brodick met his gaze with a meaning look. Neil recalled the story of the Sand Creek hanging which Dora had heard from Mrs. French and later told to him. This, then, was the thing which was between Lentu and Left Hand.

But Left Hand was speaking again in a voice that trembled with passion.

"There was a boy with those two men, Lentu, a young boy, unarmed, inexperienced, a relative of one of those men you hanged without giving a fair chance. You drove that boy out upon the prairie to die. You

229

would have killed him, too, but you couldn't find him later in the night. You thought his bones were found bleached and scattered on the prairie the next spring.

"Lentu, that boy didn't die. He wandered, frightened and starving, until he was found and taken in by the Blackfeet Indians. He lived with them for years because you had killed his faith in white men. And to this day he has hated white men—yes, and killed them—because of that hate, and because he taught himself to shoot faster than any one of them he has ever met; learned to hate and to shoot and to kill so that some day he might pay *you,* Lentu, in hot lead.

"I was that boy, Lentu, and now I am that boy grown up. I see by your eyes that you know I am speaking the truth. I'm glad, Lentu; glad you should know all this before—the end!"

The voice seemed to mellow into a plaintive tone as Left Hand finished. After a few seconds he spoke again, softly and musically, seeming to caress the words as they left his lips.

"And this is why I have come after you, Lentu. I kept track of you, and I waited until I knew you couldn't beat me in a gun play, for I had to tell you first. When the government offered me the job of putting a stop to the range troubles hereabouts I took it because it would give me a chance to get you and get you right. It was an accident that you got Swain; it would have been an accident if you had got Brodick, and you wanted to get him and seal his lips for all time. But I'm not going to get you by any accident, for you haven't got any more chance than you gave the two men you hung and that boy—myself."

Left Hand Smith took three steps toward the door leading into the refreshment room without lowering or shifting his gaze.

"I'm hoping this is the last time I'll have to use my gun," he said in a low voice as if to himself. "I'm going back up to Canada where I was born. I'm doing a real service to this country by ridding it of you, Lentu, and saving the State or government some money."

Again the interval of silence.

"Are you coming out, Lentu?"

The speaker stooped ever so slightly, gathering his muscles tense for a spring.

"Lentu, if you're not coming out, I'm coming in!"

A flashing instant of time and Left Hand's body shot into the doorway to the thunder of blazing guns. Neil scrambled through the window and with his uncle was among the first to enter the refreshment room, pungent with pistol smoke.

Lentu's body was still leaning backward against the counter. At his feet lay two guns. Left Hand leaned forward from just within the doorway as the body slipped to the floor. He broke his weapon and spilled the empty shells upon the huddled form, then slowly replaced it in the sheath on his left thigh.

The bartender rose from his place of safety, stared about awkwardly, and began wiping the counter before him in a foolish manner with his bare hands. A dog, awakened from his nap by the sound of the shooting, came from one of the deserted card rooms in the rear. From within the lobby came the sound of some one clearing his throat. Then a casual word was spoken, and soon arose the discord of excited voices.

Left Hand Smith immediately pushed his way through the crowd and disappeared.

## CHAPTER XXX
### LEFT HAND'S FAREWELL

IN the cool, sweet breezes of late afternoon Amos Brodick, Dora, and Neil rode back up the long slopes of Angel Butte in the buckboard behind the best road team on the 3-X-Z, and, in the first hour of the twilight, emerged from the cañon road to the floor of Wild Horse Valley. As Amos gave the horses free rein, and as they hurried between the fields of stubble for the main gate, the ranch bell, used to call the men to meals, was heard ringing merrily.

All the men on the place, as well as Mrs. French and the boy, Louis, came out to the gate to meet them, and Neil felt a strange lump in his throat as they shook hands with him and joshed him in the best of natures about being too tough to kill, and bullet-proof, while they congratulated him and expressed their pleasure at his recovery.

It was a royal welcome, truly Western in spirit, and while Neil felt that he hardly deserved it he mentally resolved that his future life with them would never once fail to merit their good-fellowship and confidence.

They sat down to a splendid dinner with appetites sharpened by the crisp autumn air, and then, while Dora assisted Mrs. French with the dishes and other household duties, Neil and Amos Brodick sat in the little office in the front of the ranch house. For the first time Neil told his uncle all the details connected with the killing of Swain.

With a blush of shame Neil confessed that he had at first suspected Swain, that he had not been altogether sure that Lentu was not telling him the truth, that he had feared Lentu and his veiled threat to kill him if he told all he knew, that he had at the time actually hoped that Left Hand was implicated. He bared his groundless jealousy of Left Hand and spared none of the details of his foolish thoughts and actions in which he had, as he now saw, been disloyal to his uncle and the ranch.

"I came out here with the wrong idea, Uncle Amos," said Neil earnestly. "I thought I wanted to be a gunman, and I didn't even know what a gunman was or how he was made. Left Hand's story taught me things!"

Then he explained the feeling of exultation and joy which had come over him when he saw his uncle battling with Martin before the stampeding herd and the racing fire; how a sense of loyalty and justice and right was born in him at that moment, and how he saw afterward the meanness of the combine's selfish stand against the homesteaders who had come out, veritable pioneers of an era of agriculture, to reclaim the prairie wastes.

Through it all Amos Brodick listened with sparkling eyes. When Neil had finished he laid a kindly hand on his nephew's knee.

"There was a great preacher, son, who once said in one of his sermons that 'tremendous natural scenery makes the greatest natures for good or evil'—I think that's the way it goes. An' that's sure true out here. You fell in with the evil crowd at the start, an' you can't be blamed so much. But you've learned something, an' I don't know as I would have had it any other way. Now you're on the right road with a clear track an' no more gates to open. You'll make it all right. An' now, son, we'd better go to bed. We've got work ahead of us, for we'll have to get ready to ship the beeves in a few days."

The day following Neil was plied with questions from the men who wanted all the details of the meeting between Lentu and Left Hand. Neil described the scene and repeated Left Hand's words as best he could, never without respect for the terrible seriousness which attended the merited death of Lentu.

"Served him right, an' he got just what was coming to him," declared Williams, voicing the sentiment of the others who nodded in strict approval. "An', Sterret, you know I had a hunch you was bein' fed a lot of stuff by Lentu an' his gang, an' so did Swain, but he says 'Let him go, an' if he's got any stuff in him at all he'll wise up to it himself.' An' you did, an' the crowd's with you. Put it there."

The handclasp strengthened the resolve which Neil had made.

There followed days of hard work on the ranch in which Neil participated more and more, willingly and happily, as his strength returned. The beeves were rounded up, and Amos Brodick went to The Falls and arranged for the cattle cars to be spotted on the Angel siding. Then the herd was driven to Angel and the cattle loaded into the cars, and Amos and two of the men went East with the stock to the Chicago market.

Neil and Walt Frost went on a hunting expedition and brought back two deer. The grouse on the slopes about the valley were plentiful, feeding now on the juniper berries. Plowing was under way, and there was fencing and woodcutting and hauling. The men on the place had plenty to do to get things shipshape for the long, cold Montana winter which would soon gather the land in its icy grip.

The first snows had fallen, melted in the valley and on the south slopes, and shone white upon the peaks in the warm sun of the late Indian summer when Amos Brodick and the men returned from marketing the cattle.

"Well, we're all squared off at the bank, Neil," said Amos cheerfully. "Couldn't lose out on this ranch now if we wanted to. Cattle's in fine shape for the winter, an' everything's set for a good year to come. I guess I better take you in on the secret of my books—such as they are—an' maybe you can help me a little with the figuring."

Neil laughingly waved a hand in protest. "Wait until there isn't so much outside work to do, uncle, before I have to get ink on my fingers."

Two days later Neil and Dora were sitting on the porch in the sun. They had been together more often during the weeks following Neil's convalescence. Each seemed to sense a difference in the attitude of the other. Dora was always cheerful and smiling and perhaps a bit shy, while Neil appeared subdued and serious.

So interested were they in the casual bits of conversation in which they indulged that they failed to notice the approach of a rider until he thundered up to the gate on his big black horse.

"Left Hand Smith!" cried Neil in glad surprise.

Amos Brodick came running out upon the porch and shouted a greeting to Left Hand, who dismounted and walked rapidly toward them.

"Just dropped over to say good-by," he said gravely. "Had to get my pack horse an' stuff down at Angel. I'm starting for Canada tonight."

Amos had one of the men look after the big black, and Left Hand sat down to dinner with them.

"Guess it won't hardly be necessary for any of you to go to The Falls on the McCabe and Pierson matter," he informed them. "Pierson an' some of the men made a complete confession of the whole scheme an' put the blame on Martin an' Lentu—as you know. Then McCabe an' the others pleaded guilty. They're all due to be sentenced tomorrow."

After dinner on the porch Amos Brodick looked at Left Hand with regret in his eyes. "We're right sorry to see you go, Smith," he said. "I was goin' to ask you if you wouldn't stay here an' take on the job of bein' my foreman for a time—"

Left Hand's laugh interrupted him. "No use, Brodick. I'm going back to Canada an' try to forget a lot of things, an' who knows but what I'll go to farming up there! I guess maybe you've got material for a foreman right there." He indicated Neil, who flushed under his tan at the compliment.

Left Hand advanced to Neil and, pulling a pistol from his hip pocket, offered it to him. "Here's your gun you loaned me that day up on the butte," he said, smiling.

Neil drew back. "I'd—I'd rather you took it along as—as—a keepsake," he said slowly. "I—don't want it!"

Left Hand again pocketed the gun and held out his hand. Neil took it with a joyous smile as he recognized what it meant. Then Left Hand said good-by to Dora and the others, and Amos Brodick followed him to the gate as a man brought around the big, black horse.

Dora and Neil stood arm and arm watching Amos as he bade Left Hand Smith farewell. They waved as Left Hand saluted them from the saddle and galloped up the trail toward the cañon road and Angel Butte.

They were watching him out of sight when Amos came back to the porch.

"By golly," said Amos, "I actually believe you two are gettin' kind of chummy lately."

Neil, taken aback, looked down at Dora, who lowered her eyes and blushed.

"There, now, what'd I tell you, young lady?" Amos went on in a hearty voice. "Didn't I say I'd give you two till along about Christmas. By golly, I believe I hit the mark!"

Neil turned Dora around facing him as his uncle went chuckling into the house.

"What does he mean, Dora—Christmas? I guess I'll have to start all over again after—what's happened. But if you still think that in another year I can—why what's the matter, girlie?"

Dora had thrown her arms about his neck and was crying softly. Her lips found his ear. "Maybe uncle is right," she whispered.

"What? Right about—about—"

"Christmas!" she murmured as he gathered her closely in his arms.

**Center Point Publishing**
600 Brooks Road • PO Box 1
Thorndike ME 04986-0001 USA


(207) 568-3717


US & Canada:
1 800 929-9108